Yes, Sir

PADDLE CREEK COLLEGE
BOOK TWO

HJ WELCH

Yes, Sir
Paddle Creek College Book Two

Copyright © 2023 by HJ Welch

Cover Design by Cate Ashwood

This book is a work of fiction. Names, places, and incidents are either products of the author's imagination or are used fictitiously. Any resemblance to actual events, locales, or persons, living or dead, is entirely coincidental.

All rights reserved. No part of this book may be used or reproduced in any manner whatsoever without written permission, except in the case of brief quotations embodied in critical articles and reviews.

Trigger Warning

In this book, Benedict and Jackson role-play as characters and take part in consensual non-con scenes. They talk a lot about their kink, why they enjoy it, and why with enthusiastic consent, it's absolutely okay. The tone of these scenes is generally playful and dramatically over the top, but some readers might find the language they use troubling.

Prologue

FOUR MONTHS AGO – BENEDICT

I almost escaped in time.

Almost.

"Knight!" Bobbi Schultz, the head of the department calls out to me at the end of our first faculty meeting of the school year.

I tell myself not to be grumpy as I pause on my way out the door, letting others pass me as I greet Bobbi with a smile.

"Got a sec?" she asks as she strides up to me, swinging the strap of her purse over her shoulder. As usual, she's rocking a bold colored pencil skirt and blazer, three-inch pumps, and an expression that lets you know she hasn't tolerated nonsense from anyone this side of the millennium.

"For you, always," I say with a slight nod. We both know it wasn't actually a request, but despite her frosty exterior, I do actually consider Bobbi a friend, so I'm happy to play along.

Her lips twitch in amusement before she continues marching out of the room and into the corridor.

"Are you excited for a new batch of eager minds to mold?" she asks as she click-clacks down the hall beside me.

"Of course," I say sincerely.

This is one of my favorite parts of teaching higher education. I love discovering which bright young things I'll be guiding through the next few years in their journey back through time. Naturally, things are a little different here in Paddle Creek, Indiana, compared to Oxford, England, where I taught for several years previously. But in some ways, I prefer the less elitist approach to student intake at smaller colleges.

I get a pang of sadness, thinking how I won't get to see these new students graduate. But that's just the way it has to be. Time stops for no man.

"Excellent," Bobbi says, her gaze fixed ahead as we walk toward the quad. Unfortunately, it appears she has a similar train of thought going on as me. "You know how much we value you here, Knight."

I hum, already aware of where this was going. "I know, Bobbi. But it's still going to be my last year. I've given you plenty of warning. It's time for me to go home."

She pouts as she holds the door open for us both to step through. "Really? After two years, you still don't feel at home here?"

I give my friend a sideways glance. Bobbi isn't exactly a hugsy-feelsy sort of person. Don't get me wrong. She's brilliant at her job. It's one of the things that made transferring out here more bearable. But there are times when I feel like I've met sharks with more empathy. So I try not to take her bluntness too personally.

"This was my mother's home, not mine," I say softly.

To her credit, she stops walking across the brightly lit courtyard and sighs. "Oh, Ben. I'm sorry. Of course. The faculty and students love you so much, is all I meant. You've fit right in since day one. How are things since your mother passed?"

It's my turn to sigh, and I take the opportunity to sit on a nearby bench, looking up at the clouds gently drifting along in the sky. "As good as can be expected, I suppose. Unlike with my dad, we were prepared."

Some people simply get dealt a shitty hand in life. I was a miracle baby that my parents had late in life, so it was just the three of us, but that was all we needed. Until one day fifteen years ago when Dad got knocked off his bicycle and was killed instantly. The loss broke my mother, so she returned to her childhood home here in Indiana. I was already grown and working then, so I chose to stay in England. When her cancer prognosis came through two years ago, I uprooted myself from Oxford to spend what time I could with her.

So now it's just me. And yet people are still surprised when I tell them that the plan was always to go back to the place I made my home in the UK. Why would I stay? Other than for my students.

Urgh, there's that pang again. If I could, I wouldn't take on a new class this semester. I hate the thought of abandoning them. But I'll be leaving behind the second and third years as well, so there really isn't an ideal solution.

If I'm honest, Paddle Creek is an utterly charming town, if somewhat dilapidated. All the investors flock to Albertson down the road. The proverbial Goliath to our David. But I've basically been able to build my own classics program here at the college from the ground up and handpick wonderful faculty. I know they'll be in safe hands once I go.

Remaining in Paddle Creek was simply not part of the plan. If I stay here, I can see that I'll stagnate. Besides, dear *lord* there is absolutely no kink scene anywhere close. I have to drive three hours to find a decent club, and it's all become a bit of a chore. I left a very sweet sub back in Oxford. He's since moved on with his life—as I told him he must—but I'm sure I could find someone new in no time at all once I return.

Living in a small town like this has been a struggle. No, it's been like living in a desert next to its only oasis. Thanks to the football team's out and proud coach, Paddle Creek actually attracts a high number of LGBTQIA-plus students, and there's a thriving queer community.

But not one I could ever play in.

I clear my throat, aware I've become lost in my thoughts. Bobbi is sitting beside me and is quietly admiring some birds in a nearby tree. This is one of the things I do really like about her. She may be as blunt as a spoon, but she also knows when to respect someone's privacy. We Brits are getting better on the whole at showing our feelings, but I am aware that I do suffer from a stiff upper lip, and overt displays of emotion make me extremely uncomfortable.

"Sorry about that," I say dryly.

She shrugs. "Sorry about what? Come on. Let me walk you back to your building."

Classes don't start back for another couple of days, but she knows I like to take some time in the big lecture hall to work on curriculum planning. It helps orient me. Besides, I never fully moved into the apartment I've been renting. Most of my life is still in storage back in England, waiting for me to return. Seeing the lack of home comforts around me can be bleak at times, although at least I have my dog, Dotty, for companionship. The college classrooms might also be devoid of personality, but they come to life when the students fill them. I feel like some of that energy lingers in the walls, nourishing me.

"So, if you're dead set on leaving and breaking all our hearts, I figure that means you owe me a favor," Bobbi says with a sassy edge to her voice.

"Oh, no," I can't help but utter.

Luckily, she laughs. "Oh, yes," she says smugly. "I've found you a TA."

I stop walking again, but this time it's to glare at her. "No," I say firmly, raising a finger. "I don't need a teaching assistant. I don't want one. I've told you before, it will mess with my process."

Bobbi just grins and continues walking. I roll my eyes and jog to catch up with her. "Your process can be a little slow," she says with a flick of her eyebrows. "It's your own fault. You made a department with a killer registration, and we've got more students than ever enrolled in classics this year. You should be proud! Between you and the football team, this town is finally starting to make something of itself."

"So this is your idea of a reward? Come on, then. Who are they? I assume you've already hired somebody, and my protesting is futile."

"Yes, but it's cute," she teases with a wink. "His name is Jackson Riggs."

"Jackson—oh, *god*," I say with a grimace. "I hate him already. He probably spends all his time drinking beer and banging chicks."

"Your American accent is still terrible," she says, calling me out on my impersonation of what is bound to be an insufferable young man. I know I shouldn't, but after over a decade in higher education, I've got a sixth sense when it comes to names.

Young men called things like Hunter, Maverick, Todd, Bryce, and yes, Jackson, are usually the offspring of parents who watched too many action movies in the eighties. I'm already expecting the type of toxic masculinity I utterly loathe.

"Does he know I'm gay?" I ask pointedly.

Bobbi rolls her eyes. *"He's* gay," she says. "And he also happens to be my godson, so how about you pack away some of that pride and prejudice, Jane Austen?"

I click my tongue, significantly chided. Godson? There's

not going to be any wriggling out of this, is there? "I apologize."

She chuckles. "Apology accepted. Look, I know this kid, all right? He's the son of my best friend from high school. He's smart. He majored in philosophy down in Indianapolis, and he's been doing a bunch of unpaid internships. I think he'd like to get something like an executive assistant role, but he hasn't had any luck so far. And you know my feelings on unpaid internships."

I grunt. On that, we can wholeheartedly agree. They are the work of the devil. "So you offered to pay him."

She raises her hands as we approach my building. "I know nepotism isn't great either, but I wouldn't have suggested it if I didn't think he could really help you out. He's a nice kid, Ben. You be nice, too."

"Wait," I say suspiciously, slowing down as we make our way down the familiar corridor to the main lecture hall. I look at the door. It's ajar. "He's in there, isn't he?"

Bobbi looks smug. "Just say hello," she insists as I groan. "This is happening, Knight. So you might as well enjoy the ride."

I rub my forehead. "You are a cruel woman, but I suppose it will only be until May. Nine months. I can tough it out until then."

She laughs and shakes her head. "You'd think I was tying a stone around your neck. Come on. You'll see. He's going to change your life."

"I sincerely doubt it," I grumble.

Nevertheless, I trudge behind her as she marches into my violated sanctuary. I suppose it could be worse. She could have invited him to my office. I suppress a shudder at the mere thought. At least here he doesn't have much to poke around in.

Or break.

Before I cross the threshold, I mentally brace myself and muster a smile, dreading what kind of *dude* I'm about to be faced with.

Then I stop.

He's a young man, all right. An athletic one, like I perhaps unfairly guessed from his name. The way his jeans and T-shirt cling to his muscular arms and thighs doesn't leave much to the imagination. But then he looks up from the book he's perusing, peeking through beautiful long dark lashes, and gives me the most gorgeous smile.

"Professor Knight," he says in a voice like butter.

Oh.

Oh, no.

In that moment it becomes immediately clear that this is going to be a *very* long nine months indeed.

CHAPTER 1

Jackson

"TWO STRAWBERRY DAIQUIRIS," I PRACTICALLY YELL AT THE bartender. The local favorite drag queen, Kimmi Sugar, is nailing an ABBA medley on the small stage here at Creams. As the clock creeps closer to midnight, everyone's trying to get a drink in to toast to the new year, but luckily, I'm taller and bigger than a lot of these twinks so I (nicely) squeezed my way to the front.

"Regular or virgin?" the hot, topless guy asks. If he wasn't about twenty years too young for me, I'd have tried flirting. But the poor man has probably had enough already this evening, and the night is nowhere near over yet.

"Definitely not virgin," I say with a snort.

He grins and swiftly moves to the slushie machine, where they have three flavors of daiquiris on tap in both alcoholic and non-alcoholic versions. Sure, they don't taste quite as good as freshly made ones, but they're ten times faster and half the price.

Life's too short to be spent hanging around. That's my philosophy, anyway. An opportunity comes my way—like this sweet TA gig back home in Paddle Creek—I don't overthink it. I look at my bank balance after working my ass off for free for over a year, then tell my godmother 'yes, please' and 'thank you' without hesitation. Generally, I see what I want, and I go for it, worrying about the consequences later.

Generally.

"There you go, dude," the bartender says, placing two large glasses filled with red icy goodness in front of me. I hand him a twenty, wait for my change, then ease my way through the throng back to my bestie, Selena, who's been guarding our small table like a junkyard dog. She might be tiny, but she's certainly feisty.

"Woohoo!" she cheers, wiggling her fingers in the air as she sees me and our drinks.

Her tight curls are cut extremely short and bleached blond in contrast to her dark skin. She has the kind of bee-stung lips that people pay thousands of dollars for, and they're always dripping with gloss. Her wardrobe seems to mainly consist of ripped things connected together with chains. Several piercings twinkle in her ears, and if she were to poke her tongue out, you'd see the bar running through it. I've never asked if there's anything metal between her legs or concealed in her bra, but I can take a wild guess.

I'm thankful we've been friends since middle school. Otherwise, I'm almost certain I'd never be cool enough to hang out with her now.

"Happy New Year," she cries, clinking our glasses together.

"We've got another ten minutes yet," I protest as Kimmi Sugar gets the crowd roaring and clapping along to the next song.

"Just enough time to make resolutions, then," she declares with a wink as she sucks on the paper straw.

I groan. "You know I think that's bullshit."

"Come on," she begs, smacking my arm playfully. *"You*

know I don't mean lose weight or get a promotion or any of those stupid things. I mean, new year, new energy. What are you going to do to make yourself happier? To live fuller."

I narrow my eyes at her and try not to drink my daiquiri too fast so I don't give myself brain freeze. But it's hard not to reach for a distraction. "I don't know what you're talking about," I say smoothly.

She rolls her eyes, but there's a fondness there that lets me know it's something she's doing out of love. "Really? You can't think of anything you might want to be *open* and *honest* about that might bring you joy and happiness, hmm? Maybe with a certain *someone?*"

"You're drunk!" I say with only a hint of a squeak as I reach for her glass. "You don't know what you're saying! I better take this off you!"

She giggles like a maniac and dances out of my way. "La la la, I only speak the truth," she sings.

I sigh and stir my slushy ice. She's the only person on the entire planet who knows my secret. I don't want to call it embarrassing or dirty, but I am terrified that one day I'll be found out.

Because I might not know exactly what's in her bra, but she knows that I am *wearing* a bra. Right now. She might not know the color or style, but she knows it's there, hidden away for my pleasure only.

And that's the way it's going to stay.

Guys who look like me shouldn't want to wear satin and lace. They shouldn't like the way it feels cupping firm pectorals or against their thick, hairy thighs. I look like a dude. I *am* a dude. A large, muscular one. I played basketball in high school and have been lifting weights since college.

This thing that makes me so happy doesn't make any sense. Not even to me.

Selena knows this. I only confessed it to her a couple of

years ago when I was getting seriously into it because I was honestly worried there was something fundamentally wrong with me.

After very kindly asking me if I was trans and what pronouns I wanted to use, Selena stopped being gentle and started reminding me as often as she could that I was being an insecure dumbass and that anyone worthy of being with me will love, understand, and even get off on my little kink.

I don't share her optimism, though. I've never divulged my secret with a guy in real life, but I thought I'd try online, where it felt more protected.

Ha.

The kind of messages I get on dating apps—even the new kinky one, Collr—range from incredulity to laughter to obscene threats of violence. I couldn't face someone rejecting my most intimate pleasure face to face. It would crush me.

"Yeah, maybe," I say with a shrug, lying through my teeth.

There's no way I'm going to lead a first date with 'Hey, I'm Jackson, I bench two hundred pounds, and wear a 44C cup.' The thought breaks me out in hives.

But there are times…late at night in the dark when it's safe…I fantasize that perhaps I'll meet a nice Daddy. Someone who's strong but kind and open-minded. If I got to know him well enough, in my dreams, I imagine what it might be like to reveal my secret. It's my fantasy, so in my mind, this faceless older man is shocked but also delighted in the best possible way.

I feel like I've got a better chance of finding a unicorn, though. Younger guys like me seem to be more into bending gender binaries. Hell, if I had been born twenty years ago, I would probably never have had the guts to experiment like I have. But that's the problem. I've always been attracted to older men, and they're often from a generation that like to keep the masculine and feminine separate.

Someone like me would break their brain.

I had a couple of boyfriends in high school before I got into all of this. Those relationships were mostly based on having as much sex as possible. I tried topping and bottoming, which is where things started to go 'wrong,' I guess. The last guy I was seeing basically broke up with me because I didn't want to top anymore. He said that was my whole vibe, and I suppose he wasn't wrong. Guys always assume I'm the top.

Perhaps that's what first drove me to older men. It felt more acceptable for me to want to bottom and let the older guy be in charge. I began to realize, though, that I find the wisdom and maturity that often come with age deeply attractive.

One guy I dated let me call him Daddy and seemed to enjoy looking after me, but he didn't *identify* as a Daddy. It gave me a taste for it, however. I don't mind hookups with whoever, but I'm determined my next relationship is going to involve me being a good boy for a caring Daddy. I crave it.

But then that brings me back to my problem and Selena's point. I've always worn my lingerie in secret when I'm certain I won't be discovered. I haven't dated in ages, so I've been getting bolder and wearing it more often. If I want to see someone seriously, though, they're going to need to know.

I shudder at the thought of bringing it up.

I went on a date last year with a guy and tried to broach the subject of blurring gender lines. He sneered and said he had no time for 'fucking fairies' and that if 'I wanted to fuck a woman, I'd fuck a fucking woman.'

Needless to say, I lost his number. And any scrap of confidence I'd mustered to confess my secret.

Except, I keep holding on to this fantasy of mine like an

anchor. I can't help but hope one day, someone will accept me.

But the other problem is, these days, the man in my daydreams isn't so faceless. I've never said anything, but Selena knows it.

"Just *ask* him," she pouts as she dances back over to me. "This TA thing is temporary. You said he's going back to England in the summer. What have you got to lose?"

I arch an eyebrow pointedly. "My *job*," I tell her. "Which I need for the next five months. Look, it's just a little flirting—mostly one- sided. I bat my eyelids and do anything he asks me like an eager lap dog, and I get a kick out of it. That's all. He's never shown any actual interest in me."

So, yeah. The professor I work for, Benedict Knight, is, like, seriously hot in a total Daddy-Dom way. I don't even have any idea if he's into kink or what. But he just radiates the kind of calm confidence I'm drawn to. I never should have admitted to my bestie that I like to tease him a bit.

My godmother calls him Ben, but he once told me he prefers Benedict, so of course that's how I think of him, even though he's Professor Knight in real life. Benedict. My Benedict. Urgh, I'm so hopeless.

Selena rolls her eyes. "He's *British*. Really properly British. He could be burning with desire, and all you'd see is a quirk of his lips or some shit. Like Mr. Darcy! He's never going to make a move unless you spell it out for him."

"And we're back to the part where I'd lose my job," I remind her. "I looked it up. The college is okay with faculty dating, but being a TA is different. I'm like his secretary. There's a power imbalance, and it would be seen as unethical. They're not going to fire their star professor. My mom's friend, Bobbi, says they're pretty much begging him to stay. No, I'd get it in the neck, and I'm not giving up good money right now."

She looks at me through her lashes while she sips her drink. "That's a lot of words to say 'I'm chicken shit.'"

I open my mouth to protest more, but Kimmi Sugar's voice comes over the microphone. "One minute till midnight, folks! If you're gonna kiss someone, grab them now!"

I sigh. I don't want to actually fight about this. I know Selena's only got my best interests at heart and wants me to live a fulfilled, authentic life. But I can't wish that into existence. Not even on New Year's Eve.

"Will you be my kiss?" I say in only a slightly defeated tone of voice.

She also sighs and wraps her arm around my back. "Of course, gorgeous. And I'm sorry if I pushed too hard."

I shake my head. "You didn't. I know you're right—about the honesty thing. Not about a certain British professor. I just need a little more time to find the right guy to trust, I promise."

She beams and boops our noses together. "You are amazing, and the right guy is out there for you—all of you. The only thing I ask is that when the time comes, you muster just a tiny bit of courage and don't slam the door in the face of opportunity."

I look into her big, brown eyes for a moment, then smile and nod. "I promise. Now what about your new year's resolutions?"

She scoffs as Kimmi starts leading the crowd in a chant counting down from ten. "Oh, hon. I'm already fabulous. My only resolution is to chase down *more* pussy and dick. I owe it to the world to share my awesomeness."

I laugh wholeheartedly as the clock strikes twelve. All of Creams cheers loudly as Auld Lang Syne starts playing, and several people around us lock lips in passionate kisses.

Selena and I hug tightly, years of friendship and love

transcending the need to make out. Deep down, I know she's right. I'm halfway through my twenties. I need to stop hiding who I am. But for now, I have a slightly different plan of action.

"Shots?" I suggest to her as the sound system changes back to blasting Lady Gaga.

She grins at me with her incredible smile. "Shots," she agrees.

I can tackle my new year's resolution on January second —when the hangover has subsided.

CHAPTER 2

Benedict

"ALL RIGHT, MAKE SURE YOU READ CHAPTER THIRTEEN BEFORE our next class," I call out to my Intro to Greek Lit class as they begin packing up their stuff. "Perhaps have a think about the use of nature imagery and what it might mean."

I'm happy to be back to work. The holiday period stretched out longer than usual this year. Last year, I didn't celebrate, as it was clear my mother was nearing the end of her life, and her hospice care was far more important than all the frivolity that comes with Christmas. But it meant that all the usual festive cheer this year sadly reminded me all too much of her passing. I didn't bother putting up a tree or attending any parties. I spent the day in question curled up with a good book and a nice pot of tea.

I like the brightness of the new year. There's an energy in the air that promises fresh beginnings. This will be my last year in America. Perhaps by the next holiday season, I'll find my Christmas spirit once again, back home in Oxford.

Speaking of fresh starts…

"Gabe," I call out to one of my favorite students before he can slip out of the door. I know I'm not supposed to have favorites, but it's hard not to become very fond of this earnest young man. His adoration of ancient Greek culture and mythology is something special indeed. I see an exciting future ahead of him.

But I also know he's going through some changes in his personal life, and I feel protective over him.

His face lights up as he wanders over to the desk where I'm closing down my laptop, pushing his glasses up his nose. "Yes, Professor?"

"I wanted to thank you for your paper on the role of women in Medea from the end of last semester. It was a joy to read. I especially liked your insight on the role of women in ancient Greek society at large."

He goes pink at the praise, but he's clearly thrilled. "Thank you, sir. I enjoyed writing it."

"No need to call me 'sir,'" I remind him gently. By which I mean 'please don't.' But I can't come out and say that directly in case he asks why. Luckily, he just nods.

"Oh, yeah. Sorry."

"Not at all. I also wanted to check everything was okay. My TA let me know you had a bit of a tricky situation last month."

My relationship with my handsome TA has been just as strained as I knew it would be. I probably come off as a completely cold fish from striving to feign disinterest. But discussing students and their work is a safe zone for us to have a real connection.

When Jackson told me all he'd seen regarding Gabe after one of the college team's last American football games, my heart broke for him. I made myself wait until the new year to talk to him about it so it wouldn't be so raw, but still, I see the pain flicker through him now.

His face falls ever so slightly before he musters a smile.

"Yeah, there was a little drama with my mother. But that's all over now. I spent the holidays with my boyfriends."

He's breathless as he says the last word, his eyes shining with enthusiasm and perhaps a little incredulity at his own daring. Even in this day and age, seeing a three-way relationship is pretty unusual, especially from a timid bookworm like Gabe Visoth. But I know that he's dating two of my seniors, Seth Eisen and Marty Quinn. I've noticed them following him around adoringly, carrying his books or just carrying him.

It warms my heart to see openly queer students, particularly ones in a polyamorous relationship. But it breaks my soul to know that his parents have apparently disowned him. No child deserves that, certainly not for the supposed crime of loving freely.

I feel a pang as I recall how supportive both my parents were before their passing. I miss them both terribly. But for Gabe, I manage a smile of my own.

"That's wonderful," I tell him. "I also assume they have you to thank for their improving grades?"

He beams. "I knew they had it in them. They just needed a little help."

I nod in agreement. "Well, I'm proud of all three of you. I'll see you next class?"

"You bet," he says as he moves to head out the door. "With chapter thirteen read! Well...reread. I've already gone through the entire book."

I chuckle fondly, putting the last of my notes into my bag. "Of course you have. See you later."

I check the empty hall is tidy for the next class and lecturer before heading out myself and locking the door. I've got a lunch break before my next class, but I head to my office first to drop off my bag. I've got half a plan to grab a sandwich and take a walk, but when I open my door all linear thought goes out of my head.

As usual.

"Hey, Professor Knight," Jackson says cheerfully, looking up from where he's arranging student papers on my desk. "Happy New Year."

A knot of longing tightens in my chest. It's getting harder and harder to ignore it, but I must. This young man is strictly off-limits.

"Happy new year to you, too," I say convivially as my racing pulse begins to settle.

It's always worse when I run into him when I'm not expecting to. It's like my body goes into panic mode at the mere whiff of his clean, slightly sweet aftershave or a glimpse of his perfect smile. As usual, his dark stubble is neatly trimmed and he's wearing a black button down with blue jeans that hug his muscular arse and thighs.

It's worse when we run into each other here. I might not have made much of a home in my flat aside from the presence of my long-haired dachshund, Dotty. But my office is almost a replica of my one from back in Oxford.

Naturally, there are bookcases lining all the walls, teeming with academic volumes—some of which I've authored or co-authored. Plant pots stand on every available surface along with a couple of different small antique-looking watering cans and misters. Beside my various qualification certificates, I also have framed photos of Dotty, as well as my parents and some friends from home. There are also some news articles regarding former students and their achievements. Mostly within the classic field, but I also mentored a young woman who got pretty far in a singing competition on the telly who I'm equally very proud of.

It's not like Jackson shouldn't be in here. He has his own key so he can do his job—and whether or not I'll ever admit it to Bobbi, he's made my life a hell of a lot easier—so he's welcome to come in here whenever he needs to. But seeing him among all my holiday knick-knacks and presents students have gifted me over the years is jarringly intimate.

However, the far more frightening thing is that I *like* seeing him here. It doesn't feel intrusive. It just feels right and natural.

"Did you go home for the holidays?" I ask, simply for something to say in an attempt to drag my mind out of the gutter. I'm sure I asked him back in December, but for the life of me, I can't remember what he said.

I was probably too busy watching his gorgeous mouth moving than listening to the words coming out of it because I am a terrible human being.

Dear god, it's becoming so incredibly difficult not to fantasize about him on his knees at my feet, looking up at me adoringly through those long, pretty lashes. Usually, I tend to be attracted to more delicate young men. 'Twinks' as the kids like to say these days. Pretty, smaller boys who yearn for my firm hand and harsh words to set them free.

Jackson shouldn't press my buttons. At first glance, he looks like the kind of walking embodiment of toxic masculinity that I avoid at all costs. Except it's glaringly obvious—at least to me—that there's something deeply feminine and sensual about him. I can't quite put my finger on it. I know it's not just the lashes, although those are to die for. There's something in his mannerisms that I find quite beautiful.

God, I need to survive these next few months without crossing this line. Bobbi would kill me if I messed around with her godson, for one thing. But it just wouldn't be ethical. Besides, he might flirt like it's his mission in life to make me flustered, but I have a strong suspicion that it's all just for fun. He probably does it with lots of guys, simply for kicks. He wouldn't actually be serious, I'm sure.

Probably.

"Yeah, I went home," he says cheerfully, coming around to lean on the desk to talk to me, his hands casually slipped into his pockets. "It's a few hours south, near Louisville. I came back here for New Year's, though. How about you?"

I offer him a small smile as I place my bag on my chair. I walked into that one. "Just a quiet one."

"Oh, right, sorry. You didn't go back to England?"

I shake my head. I usually don't want to talk about this stuff, but the part of me that aches to be closer to this young man is apparently in charge of my mouth right now.

"I have an uncle from my father's side who has a few kids and several grandkids. They live just outside of London, but this year they went back to India to visit his and his wife's extended families. I'll see them in the summer, though, when I move, so I saved myself the cost of flying and just stayed here." I shrug. "My mother's family have either passed away or moved from this area them-selves. Besides, I was never really close with them growing up due to the distance. Wow, sorry," I add with a chuckle. "You just asked about my Christmas, not for my whole family tree."

"No, it's nice to hear," he says, his tone genuine, which makes me think he's not just humoring me. "So your dad was Indian?"

I rest my hands on the back of my chair so I'm not just awkwardly standing there. "Well, he was British, born and raised. But his parents immigrated from Delhi, yes. My American mother met him whilst studying at university."

"The university you used to teach at, right?" he says excit-edly. "Oxford. I bet that made them proud."

A warmth spreads in my chest, both because he's right—

they would have been and were proud. But I also like that he intuited that.

"My father passed long before that, but, yes," I agree. "I like to think he'd have been ridiculously proud. Although I'm sure he'd have disapproved of me belonging to Christ Church college instead of Balliol. Those are almost like universities within the university, but also kind of like frat houses."

Jackson's blue eyes glitter as he nods at me, like everything I say is fascinating. He probably does that with everyone, but heat pools in my belly nonetheless.

"Your life sounds like an Enid Blyton novel," he says warmly. "Did you and your buddies run around solving mysteries at your boarding school? I bet there was a faithful dog hanging around as well."

I grin. "No mysteries," I assure him. "Aside from the occasional 'who stole whose biscuits' fiasco. But I did go to a weekly boarding school, so home at weekends. And yes, there was a dog. There's always a dog."

I think of my beloved floor mop waiting for me back home. I'm forever thankful that I was able to bring her with me from England so I never felt truly alone.

"Well, I, um, best be off," I say awkwardly. "I need to grab something to eat and all that."

"Oh, yeah. Me, too," Jackson says.

Damn it. Why do I think that he *likes* hanging around here with me, chatting about nonsense? My imagination, almost certainly. He's probably got plenty of friends his own age. I'm pretty positive that he's not seeing anyone from conversations we've had, but he's undoubtedly on one or more of those apps, connecting with guys. He doesn't need to entertain me.

And yet he does.

"Would you be all right to finish up the outline for that

roundtable session before tomorrow?" I add as he heads toward the door. I hate switching from casual talk to work, but I do actually need it.

Except he doesn't look annoyed or put out. In fact, he always seems to look like running around after me is some kind of treat.

I try not to tell myself that means anything. Just because he's diligent doesn't mean he's submissive. That really *is* wishful thinking. But that lust pools in my belly again as he beams at me as if I've given him a gift.

"Yes, sir," he quips. "Consider it done."

"No need for 'sir,'" I remind him gently. "Benedict is fine."

His eyes sparkle with mischief. "Whatever you say, sir." He winks and disappears out the door.

I sigh and sag against the back of my chair. I've never explicitly told him *not* to call me 'sir.' I'm sure if I did, he'd stop.

I don't want him to stop.

And that's why I'm an awful person.

I look up at the new dachshund calendar hanging from my wall that Bobbi bought me for Christmas. "How long until May?" I wonder out loud.

Too long.

If Jackson Riggs keeps up with his 'yes, sirs' and dazzling eyes, I'm going to combust before we even make it to spring.

CHAPTER 3

Jackson

"The line's long today," I comment as I squeeze into my and Selena's usual corner table at Paddle Creek's best coffeehouse. I say 'best,' but it might as well as be its only one as far as most people are concerned, myself included.

I'd never heard of the concept of a cat café until I came across Toe Beans when I moved back here last summer. My family moved down state way before it was set up. It used to be a regular old café when I was a kid, but now…

It blew my mind that there were actually places where you could go to chill out with cats, but it was even more awesome when I realized that almost all the fur babies are up for adoption as well. Apparently, the guy who runs it—some scary-looking biker dude called Nim—rehomes kitties at a staggering rate. I've wondered about taking one of the little guys home on more than one occasion, but right now I live in a dorm room so it wouldn't be practical not to mention it's against the rules.

At the moment, there's this adorable, tiny gray fluff ball watching me from a perch above. There are dozens of shelves drilled strategically into the walls so the cats can climb around. There are even a few rope bridges so they can cross overhead. But this little one seems content to sit and spy on me, their enormous blue eyes monitoring my every move.

When it became clear that I'd be staying at least until the school year was out, Selena insisted on setting us up with a monthly reservation here at the café. That seemed ridiculous to me until I realized how long it took to book in advance. Now I make sure to never miss our Saturday morning dates, no matter how hungover I might be.

Luckily, I had a quiet one last night, so I'm as fresh as a daisy and ready to dive into my maple pecan croissant and caramel latte. Selena, on the other hand still has her sunglasses on despite the fact that it's a gloomy January day, and has a double espresso in front of her as well as a rainbow-frosted cupcake the size of her head.

"Shh, not so loud," she says in response to my comment about the line.

I grin. "Good date last night?"

"Terrible, actually," she groans, sipping her drink. "He only wanted to talk about car engines, hence your girl drinking herself into oblivion."

"Ouch, sorry, hun," I say sincerely, squeezing her hand. "You could have canceled this morning. I would have understood."

She shakes her head. "Nope, uh-uh. Toe Beans Saturdays are sacred. I'll just blast the residual alcohol with carbs and caffeine, then crawl back into bed."

"After that?" I say, eyeing up her coffee grenade.

She chuckles weakly. "I think that might actually *help* me sleep at this point."

We talk about her work for a while, staying clear of the subject of her latest in a string of disastrous dates. My bestie does love a fuckboi, whether it be in male or female form.

I'm hoping she'll grow out of it, as she deserves someone who worships her, but I guess your twenties are for sleeping around, right?

I wouldn't know. It's not that I don't want to. More that I'm becoming more and more of a scaredy cat. I glance up at my little admirer, who still has their massive blue eyes glued on me. I bet they're braver than I am.

On my good days, I prefer to think of it as aggressively choosing myself over some hypothetical guy. I love the way I dress. Walking around while having my lingerie hidden away makes me feel like a superhero—ready to spring into action at any given moment with my true identity concealed just a button rip away. Except instead of saving the city, it's more intimate action I have in mind.

Of course, the problem as we discussed on New Year's is that I'm cockblocking myself. Dear *lord,* it's so long since I had a good fuck. I went on a few hookups in the fall but purposefully didn't wear anything spicy. They got the job done. I can't say I connected with any of the other guys and I felt pretty hollow afterward, but there is still something fundamentally different about getting an orgasm from someone else compared with your own hand and toys.

Anyway, like I told Selena, it's my issue, and I'll get out of my own way when I feel ready. Right now, I'm happy talking with her about her job. She works as a beautician, and absolutely loves it. She wants to own her own place someday focused on Black, queer beauty in particular. But her espresso apparently kicks in, and she whips off her sunglasses, pointing them at me with a glint in her eye.

"When are you going to go on another date?" she demands. "There's not putting yourself out there, and then there's hiding under a rock."

I roll my eyes. "I'll go find sex when I get desperate enough," I mumble, picking at my croissant.

"I'm not talking about sex," she says with a huff. "I'm talking about—Benedict!"

I shove the corner of pastry into my mouth. "You know how I feel about—"

"Hi, *Professor*," Selena says forcefully, looking over my shoulder.

My blood runs cold, and I hastily try and wipe any flakes of croissant off my face, probably failing miserably. "Professor Knight?" I squeak as I turn around in my chair.

Yup. My horribly handsome totally-not-a-Daddy boss is standing a couple of feet away, frozen, his eyes wide as he takes me in. *Shit.* I could curse Selena. He most likely just wanted to get a cup of tea and a blueberry muffin to-go—yes, I know his order, shut up—and run away. This place is packed, and he's not big on crowds. I know not all Brits are like that, but he seems *particularly* British in situations like this.

"J-Jackson," he stammers, blinking a few times as if his eyes are deceiving him. Oh, god. Could this get any more awkward?

I offer a little wave, praying to whoever might be listening that I don't have pastry on the tip of my nose. "Um, hey. Fancy seeing you here."

He looks around. "I usually try and pop in earlier on the weekends, but today got away from me."

"Well, that's just perfect," Selena says cheerfully as she slips her glasses back on and begins wrapping up the rest of her colorful muffin in an opened-up napkin. "I feel like literal trash, and my bed is calling to me. You can keep my Jackie-baby company while he finishes his latte."

"W-what—I—" But me spluttering does nothing to stop her from standing up and beaming at Benedict. I mean *Professor Knight.*

"You boys have fun," she cries with a wave of her hand before sweeping out of the door.

Kill me now.

Benedict looks between me and the now vacant chair, then glances around the bustling café at large. The line weaves through the tables near the door, which is why Selena and I prefer this one tucked in the corner. I guess maybe Benedict was trying to stay out of the way of people still waiting by coming this route.

That was his undoing.

Fuck. I'm so torn. I'm desperate for him to sit down, but I'm terrified of what I'll say if he does.

This is different than work. I love chatting with him between his classes in the lecture halls or his office, or even in the cafeteria. That feels safe and within the natural order of things. But out here in the wild it suddenly feels taboo, just like when I'd run into my school teachers in town. I know he's *not* my teacher, but there's the same kind of awkwardness.

Probably because I've got the biggest crush on him, and seeing him suddenly with his guard down takes my breath away.

At least his guard *was* down, I guess. Now he's tightened up like a clam, and I'm worried he's debating hurdling over the tables and patrons that stand between him and the door. Eventually, though, I assume he decides that it would be terrible manners to abandon me, and he eases himself into the chair opposite me like there's a bomb underneath waiting to go off.

Great. He has no interest in being here with me. It's so obvious. I know he just tolerates me at work—that's what Selena just doesn't seem to get. I know I like him. I try not to. Nothing could ever happen because it would be unethical.

But nothing's also going to happen because it's painfully obvious I'm not his type.

Just because I like older men doesn't mean he's into younger ones. Hell—he might run a mile if I tried calling him 'Daddy.' Slipping in the odd 'Sir' here and there gives me kicks, but he always brushes it off like a joke.

It's so not a joke.

Urgh. It's easy to flirt when I've got shit to do for him. I like being his good little boy, even if he has no idea. But now…we're sitting across from each other, and it feels unnervingly like a date.

Of course it's not. That would be insane.

"Is the tea here any good?" I ask, purely to break the awkward silence before it can develop too badly. "I always wonder about tea in coffeehouses—especially for a Brit. I'm sure you have pretty high tea standards."

He chuckles, sounding almost relieved. I don't blame him. Tea seems a safe enough topic. Except when he lifts his reusable to-go mug to drink from, my gaze is suddenly drawn to his lips, and that's *dangerous*. I snap my eyes back up to meet his, then decide to focus on my own cup and also take a mouthful.

"Actually," Benedict says in his soft, dreamy English accent, "I've learned to deal with a lot of variations on a standard cuppa. But I have to say the brew here is delightful. I'd be in here every day if I wasn't mindful of my budget."

I have to laugh at that. He's right. Coffeehouses in general are expensive—good for a treat—but not all the time if you can make drinks yourself. I frown, wondering *how* he makes tea. There's a hot water setting on my coffee machine. Is that it?

"How do you make it at home?"

He runs his thumb over the lid of his navy mug. I love that he's environmentally conscious and brings his own. I knew he did it at work but the fact that he brings it here as well is super cute.

"Various ways," he says in answer to my question. "If I'm in a rush, I'll just boil the kettle and drop a bag in a cup. But if I have time, I prefer to brew loose leaves in a pot."

I do my best not to sigh or bite my lip. The idea of him making a pot of tea like something out of a novel is just so romantic. I know he's older than me, but not *that* much older. Yet it's in moments like this that he gives me wartime or regency vibes. So classically British.

"That's nice," I say lamely. But he still smiles at me, and my heart skips a beat. Perhaps he doesn't *totally* hate sitting with me.

Maybe I won't have to kill Selena, after all.

"I assume that's your usual mocha with two sugars," he comments with a nod toward my mug. I still as I also look at it. He knows *my* regular order? But he never buys me coffee. He gives me cash and sends me out to fetch drinks for the both of us.

"Uh, no," I admit shyly, trying not to let my reaction show too plainly. "Caramel latte as a treat. Still two sugars, though."

I briefly dated a guy who tried to make fun of me for ordering 'girly' coffees. I got a particularly savage satisfaction out of ghosting that jerk. Still, I'm wary as I watch Benedict for his reaction. Nothing's going to stop me from enjoying the things I like, but I'd hate it if he judged me.

To my relief, he smiles softly. "Ah, a sweet tooth," he declares. "I'll remember that."

He will? Why will he remember that? Oh god, my heart is hammering, and my hands feel a little trembly all of a sudden.

"Oh, hello," he says as he looks down. I lean to the side of the table and see a black-and-white cat rubbing up against his leg. As he reaches down to pet them, they start to purr loudly.

"You've made a friend," I comment.

He grins up at me, his brown eyes sparkling. "Maybe?"

My stupid heart does a stupid, hopeful flip.

Why do I get the strong feeling that *I'm* the friend, not the cat? That's probably wishful thinking, but I'd never even dreamed I'd be sitting having coffee on a Saturday morning with my crush, talking about things completely unrelated to work.

Perhaps today is the day for wishes?

CHAPTER 4

Benedict

"Do you have plans for the rest of the day?" I ask before I can stop the words from tumbling out of my mouth. I tell myself it's a casual, innocent question and that I have no investment in his answer.

That I'm not holding my breath, hoping he'll say 'yes,' but secretly wishing he'll say 'no.' Not that I have any clue how I'll respond if he is free. What am I playing at here?

All I know is that I've been entranced watching him nibble at his croissant—clearly very conscious of not getting any flakes on his face. I've had to keep my thoughts in line and not idly daydream that if he did end up with a wayward crumb or two, I could brush them away and get to caress his face.

Bad, *bad* Benedict!

He hums and sips his sweet coffee. "Not with anyone else. I was thinking about maybe going for a walk to get some fresh air. There's a great spot just a few trolley stops away."

I scoff with a sort of pleasant incredulity. "I was delighted when I realized there was a tram network here in town. We have a few dotted about in the UK. It's more of a mainland

Europe thing. But I thought they didn't exist in the US outside of San Francisco or New Orleans."

He nods. "They're very rare. Some towns still have them, but those that do have typically modernized them. I'm pretty sure Paddle Creek's is held together with a hope and a prayer."

I chuckle. "That's pretty accurate about most things in this town, I've noticed."

"Yeah, sorry," he says, looking genuinely apologetic. "There's this whole thing with Albertson down the road. They seem to get all the funding and investments. Paddle Creek must be pretty shabby compared to a fancy place like Oxford."

I frown at him. "I apologize. I didn't mean it as an insult. I think this town has a lot of character and heart." Immediately, he looks up and beams at me, and I know I've said the right thing. "You grew up here, didn't you?"

He nods eagerly, looking around the busy café. "I sure did. My older sister and her family settled down near Louisville, so once I finished high school, my parents moved there as well to be near their grandbabies. I'm glad I got to come back here after college, though. It's still home to me. Plus, my bestie, Selena, who you just met is here. It's ideal."

Ah, I wondered who that stylish young lady was. Curious she knew my name and recognized me by sight. It makes me wonder what Jackson has been saying about me, but that just gets my hopes up that he's talking about me all the time. Anything like that would be dangerous, so I shouldn't hope for it.

I think about what he's just said. I might have become used to Paddle Creek, but I've never allowed myself to think of it as 'home.' My stay here has always been intended as a temporary one, so to think otherwise would complicate things. I have a life back in England I need to return to.

I don't want to dampen Jackson's enthusiasm, however. He's clearly very fond of the town, and I respect that. If I had roots and people here, perhaps I would fall more in love with it, too.

"Have you done much local walking or hiking?" he asks, and for a second I wonder where the question came from.

Then I recall that he said he'd been considering going on a little expedition sometime today.

It's been a very long time since talking with a young man left me flustered or nervous. I'm the Dom. Normally I exude confidence as the one in control. There's just something unassuming about Jackson that pulls the rug out from under me. I'm anxious that he's hinting at me to join him.

That's crossing a line.

But on the other hand, it's just a walk he's proposing, for crying out loud. Not a midnight orgy (although that would definitely pique my interests). I don't want to make him feel bad or seem rude by deflecting his offer. I decide for the moment just to answer his question and see where that leads us before jumping to conclusions.

"Yes, I walk a lot with my dog, Dotty," I reply warmly.

His pretty blue eyes go wide. "I forgot you have a dog," he says, breathlessly enthusiastic. "She's named after Dorothy from the Wizard of Oz, right?"

I try not to be too pleased that he remembered that. "My grandmother on my mother's side was also Dotty, so it's to honor both of them, really."

"I love that," Jackson says with a dreamy smile on his face that makes my insides squirm pleasantly. "I bet that's a great excuse to find all kinds of different trails."

It's happening before I can stop myself. The words just tumble out of my mouth…again.

"Would you like to walk her with me today?"

For a second, he just seems to go very still. Then he blinks and gives a tiny little nod. "I'd love to. But...are you sure? This isn't work."

I laugh. "I should hope not," I say. "But, yes. I'm sure. It would be nice to have some company. Dotty will be ecstatic to meet someone new."

He swallows, and I try not to study the way his Adam's apple bobs in his throat. Have I made a mistake? What am I hoping to happen here?

I don't know. But after being initially caught out at seeing my TA face to face in the wild, I just have a strong urge now not to let the moment end so soon.

"Okay, then," Jackson says, a small smile twitching at the corner of his mouth. "That sounds really nice. Thank you."

I'd be a fool to ignore that there's something going on here. I'd have expected him to be more relaxed and flirty like he usually is. But I feel a kind of friction hanging between us, and I'm afraid to examine it too closely.

Well, fuck it. It's happening now, and I can't say I'm sorry about it.

"Are you ready to head out?" I ask. I still have half my tea left, and I haven't touched my muffin, but I'd got them both to go anyway, so I don't feel like I have to sit here and finish them. Jackson looks like he's done, and now that we've committed to plans together, I kind of don't want to hang around and give either of us the chance to change our minds.

I know I'm playing with fire here. This young man has become a fantasy to me, but that's the way it has to stay. He's off-limits. However, I'm weak, and last year was a particularly shitty one for me. This is the first time I've felt a spark of fun with someone else in forever, and I'm not strong enough to deny myself it.

Jackson brushes his hands together—still worried about crumbs, I suspect—and nods. "I'm ready to go. I took the streetcar here, as parking can be tricky. I've even got good shoes on if you just wanted to travel straight there."

I grin. "Perhaps we should pick up Dotty first. But yes, then we can come right back out again."

He laughs, and I love the sound of it. I can't say I've tried to make him laugh too much over the past four months. I've been more focused on keeping my distance to protect myself. But knowing I've made him happy, even if just for a moment warms my heart.

"Yeah, a dog would probably help for a dog walk," he quips as he gets to his feet.

I follow suit, watching as he extends his hand out to a cat that I hadn't noticed on a shelf mounted above the table we've been sitting at. The gray ball of fluff shrinks away at first, but Jackson patiently keeps the backs of his fingers steady, and soon the little one leans forward to sniff them. After a moment, Jackson slowly moves to scratch behind their ears.

"Good kitty," he murmurs.

"You've also made a friend," I say, making him smile. My black-and-white cat has since gone on to wind around several other pairs of legs, but this little one stares at Jackson in awe, not going anywhere.

"They've been there since I arrived this morning," he says, looking at the tag on the pink collar. "Lizzie. Hi, Lizzie. I haven't seen you in here before."

There's a slight longing in his voice, and I raise my eyebrows. "We can stay a bit longer if you'd like to pet her?" I offer.

But then someone nearby laughs loudly, and she bolts away along a series of perches until she gets to the enclosed top of one of the tall cat trees situated around the café.

Jackson sighs and smiles. "Hopefully, she'll be here next time I pop in," he says. Then he shrugs. "Or not, I guess. I always want the cats here to get adopted. The owner is really passionate about that."

I glance over at the huge, tattooed guy currently scowling behind the counter. A perky young blonde woman is serving customers while he arranges cupcakes on the display. A tiny black kitten is poking their head out of the pocket in his apron.

I look back at Lizzie, who's now peering out from the cat tree box, her blue eyes wide but still looking at Jackson. Huh. They have the same color eyes.

Jackson turns and nods at me. "Shall we?" he says.

Part of me wants to go fetch the cat and let him have a cuddle. But cats aren't like that. They come when they're ready. So I figure there's no sense in hanging around, even if I feel like I've somehow let him down, which is ridiculous, but anyway.

"Absolutely. I'm parked just around the corner."

It's a gloomy January morning as we step outside. It might rain soon. But it feels beautiful to me as I walk side by side with Jackson along the pavement. For better or worse, I've committed to this now. I could worry about us socializing alone together, or I can enjoy it.

I'm going to choose enjoyment. Even if it's dangerous. I've been sleepwalking through this past year—maybe ever since I got to Paddle Creek.

A little danger might be just what I need to wake me up again.

CHAPTER 5

Jackson

I'M NOT SURE WHAT'S HAPPENING. ALL I KNOW IS THAT I'M IN Benedict's Toyota Prius, trying not to freak out at how close we are. I can smell his spicy cologne. I've been familiar with it for months now, but there's something totally different about us being in his car and feeling like I'm surrounded by it.

Is this a date? Why are we hanging out? He looked terrified to see me back at the café, but then he was the one who suggested we go walk his dog together.

That doesn't just mean spending more time together outside of work. That means he's taking me *to his home.*

I'm so nervous that I have to sit on my hands. I tell myself that nothing's going to happen—nothing *can* happen. But at the same time…I really don't know what he's thinking. I genuinely always assumed he was kind of indifferent to me. That he thought I was cute or amusing, but that was it.

There's something simmering between us in this moment. I can feel it as if it were a physical presence. My heart is hammering, and my cock is throbbing between my legs. I try not to get anxious, thinking about how it's wrapped in pretty blue lace right now. Benedict will never know that, though, so it's fine.

God, he's so fucking hot. He's focused on the road as he drives, chatting about a song that's playing on the radio. I'm only half listening. It's not that I'm not interested in what he has to say. It's just that I've got a rare chance to study his profile and I'm memorizing all the little details. I love his strong nose and the sexy flecks of gray in his dark hair. He's wearing a thick red scarf with a dark gray jacket, and he's giving off such big Daddy vibes I have to bite my lip and try and stop myself from projecting. Not all smoking-hot older guys are Daddies, honestly.

But he certainly looks the part.

"This is me," he remarks as he pulls off the road in front of a small apartment building. Down to the right, there's room for parking, but in front of the building is a little courtyard. I see a bubbling fountain and various different plants trailing from raised flower beds and hanging baskets. The bushes are neatly trimmed, and I spot a bird feeder hanging from a post. There aren't any flowers in bloom, but given the time of year that's not surprising. I bet it's a riot of color in summer.

I'll probably never get to see that, but it makes me smile just thinking about it anyway.

We're quiet as we exit his car. I wish I could think of something to say, but I'm so nervous. It helps that we're moving, so it's not totally awkward.

"Um, I can wait out here if you'd prefer?" I suggest as we reach the front door to the complex. Me coming into his personal space really does feel like crossing a line we can't come back from. Has he thought this through?

He gives me a funny look. A slight frown with a twitch of his lips. "I invited you here, Jackson," he says. "I wouldn't have said it if I didn't mean it. Do *you* want to come in?"

Holy fuck. If that wasn't some kind of Dom voice, I'll eat my expensive underwear.

"I'd like that," I say, my mouth dry. "Y-yes. Thank you."

He nods once. "Good."

That's settled then, I guess. He unlocks the door, then holds it open for me. *Urgh,* he's such a gentleman. I pause in the lobby, however, as I don't know where I'm going. He smiles at me before heading up the stairs, so I follow him.

We go to the third floor—which also happens to be the top—and then to the left. It's not a huge place. It looks like there are only three apartments on each floor, so it's nice and quiet. Plus, everything looks new and kind of expensive. The terracotta tiles on the floor match the vibe of the courtyard outside and give it almost a Mediterranean-type feel.

I live in the college dorms as one of the perks that came with the job. It's fine. It's certainly cheap. But it's not exactly fancy, and there's usually at least one room that thinks it's okay to party until two in the morning most nights. I can't deny that there's something already homely about Benedict's place, and I haven't even seen inside it yet.

He juggles his travel mug and muffin as he tries to get his keys out of his pocket. "Oh, let me help," I say, darting forward.

I take the tea before it can spill, but in doing so I brush my fingers against his. I swear actual electricity jolts between us, and I almost drop the damn mug anyway in my haste to yank back. But by some miracle, I keep hold of the thing, then offer Benedict a shy smile.

"Thanks," he says, his eyes flitting between my hands and my eyes. For a second, we're still, just staring at one another. Then he shivers ever so slightly before apparently remembering he was fishing for his keys a moment ago. "There we are," he says, finally pushing the right one into the lock.

Immediately, the barking starts, and I laugh. Benedict rolls his eyes.

"Are you ready?"

"Sure," I say with a grin, handing him back his mug. "Bring it on."

I know Benedict has a long-haired dachshund from the calendar and photos in his office. But I'm still not quite prepared for the adorable reddish-brown blur that hurtles toward my shins. Her legs are so tiny and her body so long it's kind of hilarious, as is the way she's barking like a fierce guard dog protecting her master. I've seen more terrifying hamsters, but she gets extra credit for effort.

"Dotty, behave," Benedict growls in that Dom voice again, and fucking hell, *I* want to behave for him. Dotty, however, doesn't seem to really give a crap. She jumps up and bounces against my knees while still yapping, then runs between the two of us. I don't think she knows who she's most excited by, her Daddy or the newcomer.

If Benedict was my Daddy, I'd be excited to see him every day, too.

Stop that, I will myself as I bend down and pet my new friend.

"Aren't you gorgeous," I remark.

Benedict scoffs. "And she knows it. Let me get her lead and a few other bits, then we can head out. Unless you need to use the loo or anything?"

I'm starting to think I have a fetish or a complex or something. Hearing Benedict use the British words for leash and bathroom should not be as hot as it is.

"I'm fine," I manage to say without stammering. So he grabs some things from a dresser near the door, encourages Dotty out, then locks his apartment up once again.

I'm kind of glad Benedict didn't insist on giving me a tour of his place. I'm pretty sure I'm playing with fire, and if I'd have seen his bedroom, I might literally have combusted. Back out into the fresh albeit cold air, I take a deep breath and try not to feel so lightheaded. Honestly, what am I? A schoolgirl with a crush on Sir?

Yes, actually. Yes, I am. It would be even more embarrassing to deny it at this point. At least it's only me I'm mortifying myself in front of.

My phone pings as we're heading back toward the car. Benedict is distracted by a very excitable Dotty, so I glance at it.

SELENA: HOW'S IT GOING?!?!?!

She's also added some highly inappropriate emojis, so I quickly exit the message before Benedict can catch a glimpse of my terrible friend's idea of humor. I really would die on the spot if he realized what kind of pathetic yearnings I was harboring.

I have a car. It's beat up, but it works. However, I mostly use it to get home to see my family or for other things out of town. The fact that Paddle Creek has its own streetcar system means that parking is less than it would be in other towns the same size, so often it's easier to hop onto a trolley than it is to drive. Besides, I never know when my hunk of crap is going to give out on me, so I prefer to risk it as little as possible.

Benedict's car is like a real grown-up's, though, definitely playing into my Daddy fantasy. I know it's hypocritical because my life is hardly impressive, but I just love it when men have their shit together. It's so attractive. I bet he's never had to say a prayer that the ignition will catch or that the brakes will survive another service. The interior is a mixture of shiny chrome and rich-smelling leather, and the damn seat under my butt is even heated.

"Sorry," he says with a grin as he glances over at me and his dog on my lap. She's wagging her long, feather-duster tail in my face, and her front paws are up on the dash as she giddily watches the world go by outside the car. "I rarely have passengers, so technically you're in her space."

I laugh and stroke her silky coat. "I'm sorry, baby girl," I say sincerely. "I'm glad my thighs could act as your footstool, however."

Benedict snorts. "You've got a job for life there, I reckon."

My heart skips a beat, even as I'm trying to tell it to calm down. Obviously, he meant it in a general sense. It's just a turn of phrase. But dear lord, does my body want to believe that he's suggesting something even just a little bit long term. Just the idea that we might walk his dog again together is enough to make me swoon.

He takes us to a dirt pull-off on one of the roads that goes out of town. I think I must have driven by here before, but I've never noticed people parked here or the trail I can see that leads into the forest now that I've stopped to look. The trees might be bare thanks to the time of year, but the way they're bowed over to make a kind of tunnel feels magical. Like we're entering another realm.

I glance over to find him beaming at me. "It's gorgeous, isn't it?" he says. "I take it for granted now, I suppose. I've probably walked here a hundred times at least. It's nice to see it through fresh eyes."

His compliment isn't specific to me, I understand. It would apply to anyone who'd come out here with him. But seeing as it's me here right now, I let it wash over me and settle with a glow in my heart regardless. I like helping him to rediscover joy in a beautiful place. I know he's been through a lot this past year with his mom passing. He deserves to find happiness in everyday things.

Once Dotty is let off her leash, she catapults down the pathway, barking at the empty trees like she's laying siege to a dark foe lurking in the shadows. I chuckle, absorbing some of her attitude. We could probably all do with some little dog energy in our lives.

I noticed that Benedict left his untouched muffin back inside his apartment and finished off the tea as we drove, leaving the mug in the car, so his hands are free now. He's wearing leather gloves, yet he still shoves them into his coat as we make our way down the dirt path, deeper into the woods. The sun is shining but weak. At least the wind is tempered by the trees.

"Is this colder than back home?" I ask. I don't really know much about Oxford or England other than what I've seen in the movies and such. It always seems to snow in the Christmas movies, but I have a suspicion that's just Hollywood at work.

He nods and tightens his scarf around his neck. "Typically, yes. Sometimes we have real cold snaps, but the temperature dips here appear to be more reliable. I should have put Dotty's coat on her."

"Do you want to turn back?" I ask, genuinely concerned. Dotty doesn't look like she's all that bothered, though. She's trotting along, sniffing and peeing on things quite happily.

Benedict shakes his head. "We'll just keep it short. She's only got little legs, after all. She doesn't need a hike."

I try not to feel disappointed. Obviously, Dotty's well-being is what's most important. But I'd kind of hoped that we could stay out here for a while at least. I don't want this surreal experience to end.

"We could huddle together like penguins for warmth," I suggest playfully, nudging my shoulder against his.

He laughs. "Who are you, David Attenborough?"

"Yes, Sir," I say, waggling my eyebrows.

He stumbles and stares at me. Heat immediately creeps up my neck as I pause as well. It must be colder here than in town, because our breaths are coming out in little steamy clouds, mingling together. It makes me realize how close we're actually standing.

"Sorry," I say slowly, feeling like my tongue is made of taffy. "You don't like being called 'Sir,' do you?"

"I…" he says.

I don't know what's happening, but it's as if the tone shifted in a heartbeat. I was just messing around, but it's like I've flicked a switch within him or something. He's staring at me as if he's never seen me before.

He's not *interested* in me, is he? He can't be. Not really. That would be insane. And yet the moment is stretching out, and he's so close in front of me. If we were just to lean forward…

Dotty's loud bark is like being dunked in a barrel of cold water. I jump backward, startled, and I'm not sure what to do but laugh. The spell is broken. Benedict laughs as well and rubs the back of his neck.

"We should, um, keep going, or she'll only tell us off some more."

"Right, yeah," I agree as we begin moving once again.

God damn it.

I never want this walk to end.

CHAPTER 6

Benedict

I'M STANDING ON THE EDGE OF A PRECIPICE, AND I HAVE A decision to make.

Pull away…or jump.

I knew this was a dangerous idea when I suggested spending the morning with Jackson, but I stupidly thought I could control myself. Then he goes and calls me *'Sir,'* and he was standing right in front of me, and it was as if I wasn't in control of my own body or mind anymore.

I wanted to devour him.

Thank goodness Dotty snapped me out of it before I could get myself in serious trouble, but he's no doubt noticed something weird going on. The problem is I'm truly starting to believe that his flirting has at least some sincerity behind it. If we were just casual acquaintances, I might be tempted to act on it, even just for some vanilla fun.

But *he works for me.* The closest thing I have to a best friend in this town is his godmother. And he keeps turning me on with the one thing I try and fight the hardest against, especially in this small town.

It's one thing to have someone from a club in a scene

47

calling me 'Sir,' desperate to fulfill my every whim while I fuck them senseless. But *I'm a bloody teacher.* If anyone ever found out in my real life, they might jump to the wrong conclusions. I have never, ever desired a student. Of course not. That would be seriously wrong—even at a university level. But regular people don't always understand kink, and if anyone ever thought I was a danger to them or their children...

I stumble, and I don't know if it's a blessing or a curse, but Jackson is right there to steady me.

"Benedict, are you all right?" he asks completely sincerely as he grabs my arm and looks me in the eyes. There's no hiding from him in that moment.

I look down at Dotty. She's going to be hellish later without a proper walk now, but I really am concerned that she doesn't have her coat. I think it's perhaps best after this new development if this social experiment is brought to an end as soon as possible.

I lick my lips, cold from the winter air, and shake my head. "I think maybe I shouldn't have skipped breakfast. Would you mind if we headed back to the car?"

He also shakes his head, his pretty blue eyes wide with concern. "Of course not," he says earnestly. "Are you okay to walk? I can drive if you need me to."

I swallow, feeling every bit the idiotic moron that I am. This is my own fault that I've landed in this unacceptable situation, and now I'm going to get myself out of it.

"I'm all right, thank you," I assure him, reluctantly pulling away from his strong grip. "But I think sitting down and warming up might be the best course of action."

We're a heavy kind of quiet as we make our way back to the car down the winding forest path. Even Dotty must sense something is amiss as she trots silently by my feet, looking up occasionally to see if I'm still with her.

At least I won't be alone this afternoon when I'm dying of embarrassment. She gives very good cuddles, especially when she senses something's wrong, like with my mum last year.

I'll take awkwardness as my punishment for dragging Jackson into this situation, though. I never should have encouraged anything between us. Cool politeness might be rude, but it's safe. We both need protecting from me right now.

"I'm sorry," I say again as we slip into the Toyota. Dotty jumps into the back seat and curls up, staying away from the weirdness that's replaced the electricity that was crackling between me and Jackson.

He closes the passenger side door behind him, then frowns at me. "Don't be sorry," he says kindly. "It's good you asked for what you needed."

Fucking hell. Who's supposed to be the Dom here? It doesn't matter if Jackson is submissive or not. I'm the one who should be in charge and have my shit together. Instead, I'm losing it like some romantic heroine in desperate need of a fainting couch.

I'm mortified and not quite sure what to say, so I start the engine and get us back onto the road. "Shall I take you home?" I ask.

"Only if it's on your way," he says with a kind smile. "I'm in the campus dorms."

I know that already, but I just nod in response and pull out onto the road. It doesn't feel right in this moment to broadcast how much I've paid attention to details about his life.

The Bluetooth on my phone automatically connects to my car's sound system, so quiet music thankfully saves us from a completely awkward silence. I feel myself calming down as I realize that, really, everything is okay. Nothing bad actually happened, and I've now taken control of the situation. That always makes things better.

I'm in charge. This is fine. We'll just go back to the way things were before. I'll survive until May, and then I'll be on my way back to Oxford where there will be ten times more room to keep work life and kink life separate. I'm sure I'll find a sub to play with in no time.

The thought crosses my mind that the sub won't be Jackson, and it slashes through my heart. But I grip the steering wheel tighter and banish it. No, it won't. This is just a silly infatuation. Out of sight, out of mind. I'll be fine with some space and time between us.

I pull over on one of the side streets that leads to Jackson's dorm. It occurs to me that I never asked which building was specifically his, but if he's noticed that I knew already, he doesn't say anything.

Not about that, anyway.

"I'm sorry if I made you uncomfortable," he says in a small, sad voice as he unbuckles his seat belt.

That snaps me from my funk like I've been struck by lightning. Before he can reach for the door handle, my hand darts out and grabs his arm. He turns immediately to look at me with wide eyes.

I shake my head. "No, no," I say emphatically. "You didn't make me uncomfortable. This is all my fault. *I'm* sorry."

He licks his lips, and my insides squirm. God, I want to kiss them so desperately.

"Why would you be sorry?" he asks. "I'm the one who keeps calling you that stupid name that obviously upsets you. I thought I was just teasing, but I clearly crossed a line, and I feel horrible about it. I hope we can still be friends and things won't be weird on Monday."

He gives a hollow laugh, but I'm busy spiraling. *Fuck!* I can't have him blaming himself, but I can't explain either.

Not without confessing my secret. In the pause that stretches out I grip tighter onto his arm, rubbing my thumb against his coat. I probably shouldn't do that, but I have to comfort him somehow.

"I promise you, that's not it," I say, even though it kind of is.

But it's not *his* fault those two words elicit a particular response in me, especially—apparently—when it comes out of his mouth. Dear lord, I want him uttering them reverently at my feet so badly it almost makes me shiver. I manage to control myself, just about.

But he's looking at me so earnestly, and my hand is still on his arm. He shifts his weight to face me better, and his eyes flicker, like he's thinking hard on something. Perhaps making up his mind.

"No," he says softly, shaking his head again. "I know I'm making things difficult, and I think you're owed an explanation as to why. I…I like you, Benedict. A lot. I thought maybe you were going to kiss me in the forest just now. But that's obviously not what you want, and it's unethical anyway with work. If you want me to transfer to a different department or something, I'd understand. But…yeah. That's what I'm thinking right now, and I really am sorry if that's made things a whole lot worse."

My brain is stuck, like a vinyl record with a jumping needle. Did this beautiful boy just confess to being attracted to me? Am I dreaming?

He also rightly pointed out one of the reasons why it would be wrong, but I really couldn't give a fuck about that in this moment.

"I should go," he mumbles, dropping his head and finally pulling away from me.

At least he tries to.

"No!" I cry, wrapping my hand tighter around his thick

bicep and practically yanking him back toward me. I'm breathing heavily, and for a second, we just stare at one another. "Don't go. Thank you. For telling me that, I mean. And no, I don't want you to transfer."

He raises his eyebrows. "So where does that leave us?" he asks softly. "You can forget I said any of that, and we can just go back to how things were," he suggests.

He's offering a way out. I know I should take it.

But I can't.

I jump off the cliff.

I don't know if the parachute will open or not.

"I wanted to kiss you in the woods," I rasp, but then I shake my head, feeling dizzy and lightheaded. "I wanted to kiss you the moment I laid eyes on you."

His mouth drops open. It's abundantly clear that the electricity is back between us, and it's more powerful than ever. It's like we're sitting on a powder keg that's one spark away from exploding.

His chest is rising and falling rapidly, and his pupils are dilated.

"Kiss me now," he whispers.

Boom.

I lunge for him, yanking him toward me with the hand on his arm. The other hand wraps around his neck as our mouths crash together, and I thrust my tongue against his, tasting the sweet coffee still lingering on his lips. He grabs my coat and hauls me against him, and I curse the handbrake between the two car seats. I want to drag him into my lap, but instead, I settle for letting go of his arm and slipping it past his open parka and under his soft jumper, desperate to feel the blazing hot skin underneath. I skim upward with half a plan to play with his nipple…

But then he jolts away from me like he's been burned.

My heart stops.

"S-sorry," he stammers, shaking his head and fumbling with the car door. "I can't…I mean…I'm so sorry."

He hooks his thumb against the handle and pulls, practically tumbling out of the car.

"I'm so sorry," he says again.

Then he runs out of sight.

CHAPTER 7

Jackson

I'm NOT USUALLY A DRAMATIC PERSON. THAT'S NORMALLY Selena's department. But I have a sneaking suspicion that in this instance my life might actually be over.

Since I ran back into my room about an hour ago, I've been hiding under my duvet, willing the universe to smite me down so I don't have to live with this humiliation.

I got what I so desperately wanted, for fuck's sake! Benedict *kissed* me. He said he wanted to kiss me from the moment he laid eyes on me! It was like a dream come true!

Until he slipped his hand under my sweater, and I remembered just in time what he was going to find there.

It was a mistake. We both know this shouldn't have happened. But now he's going to think I'm a lunatic. I was the one who begged him to kiss me, then I shot out of his car like I'd been electrocuted after barely a minute of making out.

I grit my teeth as my cheeks heat up with fresh embarrassment. How the hell am I going to face him on Monday? I'll have to text him to try and explain…something.

Or maybe just talk to Bobbi about transferring departments and try to never look Benedict Knight in the eyes again for as long as I live.

My phone dings and snaps me back to my senses. I'm really hot, and it's not just from being mortified. I thought to kick my shoes off, but I'm still wearing my damned coat under the bed covers. I throw them back and take in a deep breath of relatively cool air.

"Fucking idiot," I mutter to myself as I sit up to shrug off the parka. Then I fish my phone from my pocket. I expect it to be Selena looking for an update again, which would have been bad enough. But it's Benedict.

I think that's worse.

I bite my lip and unlock the screen to read the message in full. It's crazy to me that our conversations beforehand are all so inane. We talked about photocopying and lunch orders, for crying out loud.

This new message is five times longer than anything I've ever gotten from him before. I also note the time and realize I've actually only been back in my room for fifteen minutes at most, so I probably left him about twenty minutes ago. Is he still sitting out in his car? Did he drive home? Anxiety churns inside me, and I figure it's best to just read the message and get this over with.

BENEDICT: Jackson, I don't know what to say. I'm so sorry. I clearly fucked up, but I'm desperate to make it right with you. Can we talk? You can call me if you want. Or I could come see you. I know you asked me to kiss you, but it's totally fine if you changed your mind. I just need to make sure you're okay and in a good mental state. I'm more than a little worried.

He's added a smiley face with a drop of sweat at the end, and my heart pangs. I don't want him to be fretting or feeling responsible for what happened. Fuck—he was the one who was stressed, and then I flipped out. This is all such a mess.

But maybe he doesn't hate me.

The overriding tone of his message is concern. It's quite Daddyish of him, if I'm honest.

I shake my head. I can't be thinking like that now. There's already too much else going on.

I start by texting back.

JACKSON: I'm okay

JACKSON: I'm also sorry

JACKSON: Maybe talking would be a good idea

I chew my lip, watching the screen anxiously as the bubbles appear, indicating he's writing back. He begins with a crying with laughter emoji.

BENEDICT: We should both probably stop apologizing. Clearly there's been some miscommunication. But I meant what I said. I really like you, Jackson. If I didn't monumentally fuck up and you still like me, I'd want to call you or have you over here for dinner.

My heart flutters. After the way I behaved he's still offering dinner as an option? Wow.

JACKSON: Can I call you now?

BENEDICT: Of course

I take a deep, shaky breath, then go into his contact details. The phone rings once as I press it to my ear, but then he's already picking up.

"Hi," he says warmly, and I melt just a little.

"Hi," I say back. I twist a handful of bedsheets, feeling small and vulnerable.

"Are you okay?"

Of course that's the first thing he asks. I sigh. "Yeah," I say honestly. "Humiliated, but okay, I guess."

"No," he says softly yet firmly. "Please don't be embarrassed. Something obviously triggered you quite badly, and my only concern is dealing with the aftermath of that and ensuring I never, ever do whatever it was again. Can you tell me about it?"

I swallow, not sure what to say to that. He's really not mad? He just wants to look after me?

That's so nice.

But how do I answer his question? I give myself a moment by snuggling back down on my bed, wrapping the duvet up around me.

"It's hard to explain," I start off. "But you didn't do anything wrong, I promise. I…I was so happy you kissed me."

"Yeah?" he asks.

I can practically hear the smile in his voice, and for a second, I wish we'd video called instead. Or that we were talking in person. I'm still frightened of fucking this tiny blossoming thing up before it's even had a chance to bloom. But I also really, *really* liked Benedict's strong hand gripping my arm and seeing every flicker of emotion on his face. I want to read his body language and make sure we're actually communicating now.

"Yeah," I tell him back. "It's me. I have a…thing."

He's quiet for a moment. I try not to get anxious, and tell myself that it's good that he's properly listening to me, not just steamrolling over what I'm saying. I mean, he hasn't called me a freak or a cocktease like I feared, so I'm already winning.

"Is it something we can work on?" he asks carefully.

I bite my lip, Selena's voice echoing in my head, telling me that my kink is *nothing* to be ashamed of and that the right guy will be fine with it. Maybe even go crazy for it.

"Maybe," I say, my voice small. "I don't know. It's…it's something personal about me that you might not like. I'm worried you'll judge me."

He lets out a breath, and I swear it sounds like relief.

"Does this something of yours hurt other people?" he asks.

I choke and splutter. "No! No, nothing like that. It's just private."

"Ahh," he says, again sounding warm and perhaps even pleased. "Well…I still feel the same, Jackson. I like you enormously. I want to respect your wishes, but at the same time, after that kiss, I'm not sure I can just leave these feelings hanging. Would you feel comfortable talking to me more about your private matter? Then I could maybe make my own mind up about whether or not I like it. I can say with a lot of confidence if it's not hurting anyone else or problematic, I'm not going to judge you. I've seen a lot."

A full-body shiver runs over me. What does *that* mean? Is he kinky too? Holy fuck. I try not to get my hopes up, but that would be right out of my wildest fantasies if it were true.

"You have?" I ask hopefully.

He hums in affirmation. "I really have. Would you feel more confident talking over the phone about it or in person?"

I'm trembling. Am I really going to do this? What if I tell him about what's hidden under my clothes and it backfires?

What if it doesn't?

I'll need to see the look on his face to know for sure.

"In person," I say quietly. "If that's okay?"

"Of course it is," he assures me. "Would you like me to come and pick you up?"

I open my mouth to tell him that it's fine, that I can drive or get the trolley. But fuck it all to hell. I don't know what Benedict's specifics are, but he's hinted that he's not going to be easily fazed.

Maybe I can be cheeky and sneak in a little Daddying from him.

"Um, could you pick me up?"

"Absolutely," he says with clear enthusiasm, so I don't feel too guilty. I've seen how he is with the students, after all. He's obviously the kind of man who feels good helping other people. That might not be a kink, but it's at least in the right direction.

"I can meet you back where you dropped me off just now?" I suggest. *Where I fled from you,* is what I really mean, but he doesn't pass comment on it.

"Perfect. I'll see you in ten minutes."

We close the call, and I just stare at my wall for a moment. Okay, so maybe my life isn't totally over, and this isn't a complete disaster. But I still have a decision to make.

Do I get changed?

My knee-jerk reaction is yes. I want to feel safe. But… then I reconsider. I want to feel *confident.* There's a chance this could turn out better than I hope, and if we start making out, do I really want to lie to him? I think of Selena. Do I want him to see the real me and accept me for who I am?

I bite my thumbnail and roll over the arguments in my mind. If this does go further than today, I don't want to have to stop wearing all my beautiful lingerie any time there's a possibility we might make out. I want to be free.

So is that my answer? Confess my secret and hope that Benedict accepts it?

Or is the more important question: 'Do I want to take this any further if that means hiding the truth from him?'

No. I don't want that.

Fuck. That means I really am doing this. I'm going to be brave, whatever the consequences.

I'm finally going to reveal my secret. Benedict feels like the right man to share it with.

I'm scared that he won't like it, but there's a tiny flicker of optimism in my heart. Because no matter what happens, I'm sure he won't be *cruel* about it.

And that's all I can really hope for right now.

CHAPTER 8
Benedict

Jackson is quiet the entire drive back to my place, but he seems less tense, so I take it as a win. Every time I glance over at him, he gives me a shy little smile that melts my heart. I think my instincts might be right. Whether he's aware of it or not, his nature appears pretty submissive. I love that he wanted me to come pick him up. I wonder if he knows how happy that made me to be able to do that for him.

That only feeds my appetite, but I know we have a lot to work through before we can move anywhere near that direction.

I chat mindlessly about Dotty during the short drive. I tell a couple of stories about her antics, like the time she managed to bury under the fence of the apartment building's back garden. I found her a couple of frantic hours later, curled up in the lap of a charming older lady from the retirement community next door. To this day, Mrs. Brummel will pop over with home-baked dog-safe cookies for my little Houdini. I'll miss her when we move back to England.

Rather than dwell on that, I appreciate the sound of Jackson's laughter, relieved that I'm able to lighten his mood. He scared me half to death when he ran away from me earlier, but now I'm harboring a glimmer of hope.

The way he talked about something private has given me a hunch. Nothing solid, but I'm wondering if it's something kinky. He could even be trans if he'd started transitioning early. That would be absolutely fine with me, but he wouldn't be the first partner who freaked out because he was worried what was in their pants wouldn't match my expectations. Like I give a shit about that kind of thing.

All I care about is his well-being. Yes, I want to pin him down and make him take my cock and for him to beg me to let him come. But I also want to just hold him and make him feel better. I want to chase his demons away. Until today, I wasn't aware he had any. He seems so confident and happy-go-lucky. But I guess most people have a lot more going on under the surface than a casual observer would assume.

I park up the car and lead him to my door, the déjà vu strong from earlier. But this time I'm fully intending on bringing him inside my home, and there's a possibility something significant could happen there. I'm tingling in anticipation.

But I swallow down all my fears and excitement. This young man is looking to me for guidance, and I intend to give it to him. Even if just as a friend. It's occurred to me that whatever his secret is could be a massive turn-off for me. It's unlikely, but I'm braced for the possibility. The only thing that matters now is reassuring him and soothing this raw friction that's sprung up between us.

"Do you want anything to drink?" I offer as we come through the door. Dotty is just as excited to see Jackson again, but at least she keeps her barking down as she jumps all over his shins.

I reach out to take the coat he's removing. He gives it to me, our fingers brushing and sending shivers down my spine. I can tell he feels it too by the way his mouth drops open and he blinks. "Um, maybe a glass of water?" he suggests.

I'd prefer he just said what he wanted rather than asking for it, but we're not there yet, if we'll ever be. I just nod at his politeness and walk with him down the hall toward the open-plan kitchen and living room. I'd been planning on making tea, but getting us both glasses of water is much faster, so I settle on that for now.

"Please, take a seat," I say as I open up the cupboard I need, jerking my head toward the sofa. It will feel more casual there compared to the dining table, which could end up giving off interrogation or interview vibes.

He kicks his shoes off and seats himself on the end of the couch, folding his legs up against his chest. Defensive. Vulnerable.

Bollocks.

Well, this isn't going to be fixed instantly, so I just have to respect if that helps him feel more at ease, and hope we can work past it. Besides, it's pretty adorable how Dotty jumps up via her little stairs I have set up by the sofa (and also by the bed) and marches all over him until he laughs and gives her the attention she's craving.

"Oh, hello. I see. You're the boss, are you?"

"All day, every day," I quip with a grin as I walk across the room and join him. He takes his glass and has a sip before placing it down on a coaster on the coffee table.

I do the same as Dotty trots over to me, her tail wagging. "Good girl," I tell her, ruffling behind her ears. "Why don't you go lie down? Let Daddy talk to his friend."

I feel more than see Jackson go stiff. I try not to react, instead watching my little dog hop down and go settle in her basket. But when I glance up, Jackson's eyes are still wide. He gives a small shake and a smile, apparently throwing off whatever funk came over him.

Was it me taking away the safety buffer between us of Dotty's presence? Was it me calling him my friend?

Or was it 'Daddy'?

Interesting. I make a mental note for later. I think there's more and more to this young man that I just wasn't prepared for.

"How are you feeling?" I ask simply. At least, it's a simple question. The answer might be more difficult to come by, but I'm more than willing to give Jackson all the time and space he needs.

He inhales, then exhales slowly. "I'm still horrified that I reacted the way I did," he admits. "Especially after you were the one stressing out. But I'm glad I'm here. Thank you for texting me."

I nod. "Of course. It's my pleasure."

He's a fine, masculine man, but there's something small about the way he hugs his knees and plays with the toggles on his hoodie. My heart aches. I've always felt a strong attraction to him but it's funny to me how I could have ever thought that he wasn't my type.

He sighs, sounding defeated. "I suppose you want to know why I lost my shit over some perfectly acceptable PG-13 making out."

I tilt my head. "I want to talk about whatever might help you," I say. "I'm a grown-up. I tie my own shoes and everything. It takes quite a lot to upset me."

That gets the laugh out of him I was fishing for. It's quiet, but it's still a victory.

He licks his lips and looks away. "I've never told anyone about this apart from my best friend."

I can't help the slight, sharp breath I take. Well, then. This is more special, more intimate than I'd imagined.

"You don't have to tell me anything," I remind him.

He swallows, his Adam's apple bobbling, and sneaks a look back at me before focusing on his feet. "I think I want to," he mumbles.

For a moment, I don't say anything, trying to give him a moment to compose himself. Then he screws up his eyes and yanks the neck of his jumper aside. It takes a couple of seconds for me to realize what's just happened.

There's a strap lying vertically against his collarbone. It's teal blue, and as I lean closer, I can see it's lace over satin.

It's a bra strap.

I feel my eyebrows shoot up as I quickly put the pieces together.

He's wearing lingerie.

Holy fucking shit, the relief is immense. Oh, my sweet summer child. *This* is what had you so terrified? This is absolutely fine.

This is bloody hot, actually.

"Oh, hello," I say softly. "May I?"

He peeks out from under his lashes, blinking when he realizes I've moved closer to him on the sofa. Then his gaze darts to where I've lifted my hand toward his chest, and his eyes go wider.

"Yes?" he says, sounding uncertain.

Maybe he's not clear what I want. Or maybe he's surprised by my reaction. Either way, I move slowly, giving him plenty of time to pull back or tell me to stop. But he just watches, mesmerized, as I reach out, then gently stroke my index finger against the blue material.

His eyes drop closed again, and he trembles, which sends a bolt of lust directly to my dick.

"Are you wearing anything else?" I ask, my voice low and commanding. I want to know every tiny, delicious detail.

He nods, his eyes still closed. His lips are wet as he pants shallow breaths.

"Tell me," I command.

"A thong," he says quickly, like he's afraid he'll chicken out if he doesn't speak immediately. "Garters."

I run two of my fingers up and down the strap, stroking the skin beside it as well. "And do they match this pretty material here?"

He blinks his eyes open, still looking like a deer in headlights, but his gaze finds mine, and this time, he doesn't look away.

"Yes." He swallows, and I think he's digging for that courage again. "I always wear matching sets."

My heart picks up a notch. "Do you wear this all the time?" I murmur. "A pretty little secret that only you know about?"

"Yes," he whispers.

"Do you wear it when you're working for me?" I push further, leaning in closer. "When you're at my beck and call, doing my bidding?"

He studies me a second, then...

"Yes, Sir."

I don't even think. This time, I hurtle myself off the cliff, not caring if there's a parachute or not. I crash my mouth into his, surging my body on top of his, but leaving enough room to get my hand under his hoodie again.

This time, he lets me.

I quickly slide against his hard abs until I cup and squeeze his ample pec, encased in the sensual satin and lace. He moans into my mouth, grabbing the back of my neck and dragging me even closer to him.

The secret's out, and now that we're in the clear, he wants this. Wants me. Badly.

I'm okay with that. A little too okay as he whimpers and

scratches at my back through my shirt. *"Yes, Sir,"* he whines. "Take me. I'm ready for you."

"Good boy," I growl, nipping at his lip before I grab the hem of his hoodie, yanking it and the T-shirt underneath it up over his head and throwing it onto the carpet.

Fuck. His tits look sensational wrapped up like a present in the gorgeous bra he's got on. I can see his hardening nipples under the scraps of material, and I can't help but pinch the right one hard as I prop myself up with my other hand and kiss him savagely.

"Such a naughty boy," I try out. "Were you teasing Sir with your pretties all this time?"

"Yes, Sir," he gasps, thrusting his crotch against my thigh. "I was wearing it every day for you. I'm such a bad little slut. But…but I knew you'd like it."

The role play is so effortless to drop into I forget all my guarded inhibitions. This is more than I ever could have fantasized about from him. I'm delirious with need and desire, like a caveman ravaging his conquest.

"Oh, Sir loves pretty little sluts," I snarl before I bite his ear. "Especially if they need to improve their failing grades."

He gasps and even places his hand on his chest like he's so innocent. "But Sir! I need that A! Is there *any way* I can change your mind?"

I grope between his legs, feeling his rock-hard length through his jeans. "I don't know. Why don't you put on a little show for Teacher? Show Sir how badly you want that grade changed."

He pushes me back, taking me by surprise and reminding me how strong he is. That he's a fully grown, virile man. Now he's crowding over me, looking at me with such raw hunger it's breathtaking. "I'll be so good for Teacher," he purrs. "You just relax."

He stands up, and I watch as he slowly pops the button on

his jeans. Thankfully, Dotty has made herself scarce, so we don't have an audience. It's just the two of us in the whole damn world.

I reposition myself so I can spread my legs and start stroking my thickening cock through my trousers. His gaze doesn't leave mine as he drags the zipper down, then slowly pulls his jeans over his thighs.

I inhale sharply, drinking in the dark hair on his creamy legs and the teal lace strung along them. His cock fills the pouch at the front of the underwear clearly designed for men, the suspenders drawing my attention even more to it. He's a gift meant just for me, all wrapped up with a pretty bow.

And it really *is* just for me. He said he'd never told anyone about this, let alone shown another man.

Lucky, lucky me.

"Fucking gorgeous," I utter as he kicks away the jeans and socks, leaving him just in the lingerie. I squeeze my dick, trying to decide what I want—what I *need* him to do.

What I need him to do *first.*

He runs his hands down his body, looking at me coyly. "Am I pretty for Sir?" he asks breathlessly. "Do you like it? Is it good enough to get me that A?"

I bite my lip and crook my finger at him. "Not yet. I know what little sluts like you want. What's good for you. Come here and let me teach you a lesson."

I expect him to walk back over to me, but he drops to his knees and *fucking crawls.* I catch my breath and squeeze myself hard. He looks absolutely edible as he keeps his eyes on me, crossing over my rug until he reaches the sofa. Then he places his hands on my knees and batts his eyelashes at me.

"I'll be so good, Sir. I promise," he rasps.

I reach forward and rub my thumb against his lower lip.

He captures it and sucks it filthily, teasing me with what's to come.

"Good boy," I murmur, but in that moment, it doesn't feel right. "Good girl," I try instead, taking a gamble.

It pays off.

He moans, and his eyes flutter shut. "I'm a good girl," he whispers. "A pretty little slut for Sir."

I only allow myself a moment of triumph before committing fully back to the scene. "Take out my cock, naughty girl. If you want to pass my class, you're going to have to earn it."

Jackson blinks his eyes open again, looking eager to please. I'm not sure if I should switch to female pronouns, but that requires more thought than I'm capable of in this moment, so he remains male to me in that regard as he slides his hands up my thighs like a cat waiting to pounce.

"Good girl," I urge him. "You know what to do. You know what Sir likes."

In my fantasy, the teacher has been blackmailing his hottest student for months now, demanding sex whenever he wants it. And she's *so* desperate to give it to him. Such a needy, pretty slut.

Jackson confidently attacks my fly, pulling out my cock through my briefs. He wastes no time in swallowing me down deep, wrapping his hand around the base to pleasure me from root to tip.

I cry out and buck my hips, loving how that makes my gorgeous sub choke. His whole reason for being in this moment is to do my bidding. To worship me. I slide my hand through his dark hair, gripping hard and making him whimper. He's so fucking beautiful.

My breaths are ragged and fast. Adrenaline is coursing through me, making my heart hammer in my chest and my cock throb in Jackson's hot, tight throat. He guzzles me down with gusto, moaning loudly.

"That's it," I bite out as my climax starts to peak. It was never going to take long with all this explosive buildup. "Take it, you little slut. Such a good girl for Sir."

He wails and sucks harder. I gnash my teeth, chasing my release, yanking on his hair because right now, this exquisite sub is *mine.*

With a roar, I start to come. I hold his head in place, making him swallow it all. He takes it so perfectly, even as he coughs, and it dribbles down his chin. He stays the course, though, milking every last drop from me.

As soon as the room comes back into focus, I lunge forward off the couch, knocking him onto his back and pinning him down. I hold his throat with one hand, using the other to fish into his thong, pulling him free so I can start jerking him off roughly.

He seizes my shoulders as I kiss him messily. "Such a big dick for such a pretty girl. You wanted me to find it, didn't you? That's why you failed on purpose. So desperate for Teacher to fuck your brains out."

"Yes!" he howls, his face all scrunched up. "Yes, Sir! I'm such a slut for you. I can't help it!"

"Come for me, good girl," I command. "Come all over your pretty things. Show me how badly you want it."

I stroke him hard and fast until he suddenly arches his back. Thick, white ropes spurt all over the dark hair on his pale chest and the stunning blue satin and lace that frames his torso. I slow down but keep my hand moving, determined to wring every drop of pleasure from his beautiful body.

As he looks like he's coming back down, I tuck his length away again, then lean down and capture his mouth for a passionate kiss, feeling grateful and satisfied and powerful. It's been a ridiculous amount of time since I've been able to properly scene like that.

Because I'm not supposed to.

The thought hits me like a ton of bricks.

I'm not supposed to give in to those urges unless I'm under very specific circumstances. Unless I'm protected by anonymity. Unless I'm safe.

Yet I just lived out one of my favorite kinds of filthy student/teacher fantasies with my *fucking TA.*

What the hell have I done?

CHAPTER 9

Jackson

I see the moment the regret hits Benedict, and his eyes go wide with horror.

Fuck.

I only have time to think 'This isn't fair!' before he pulls back and covers his mouth with his hands.

Nope. I'm not having that. That was easily the best sex of my life, and whatever he's feeling right now, we can talk it through, like he did with my lingerie.

God. I feel like I just came out all over again, and it felt *so good.* At least it did until right now.

"Hey, hey," I say like I'm dealing with one of the timid cats at Toe Beans. I reach up and gently wrap my hands around his wrists, encouraging him to lower them from his face. "Are you okay?"

He swallows, his eyes darting around until he apparently realizes that he's still hanging out of his pants. He yanks away from my grip to shove his softening cock away and zip himself up. Then he rocks back and snatches a blanket that's draped over his couch, unfolding it with an expert flick of the wrist before carefully draping it over my shoulders.

It's such a tender act but utterly ruined by his next words. "I shouldn't have done that."

Crushed doesn't even cover it. I try and swallow the lump of emotion that rises in my throat, but it's big.

"Oh," is all I can think to say.

Humiliation washes over me for the second time that day. I've *never* thrown myself into a scene like that before. I've been submissive and called a slut, but I've never been anyone's good, pretty girl. I've never played a role and felt such an incredible rush of endorphins at the escapism. I loved every second of what just happened.

I guess Benedict doesn't feel the same way.

"I'm sorry," I say, closing my eyes so I don't have to see the pain on his face.

But he grips my chin tightly. "No! Jackson, no. Open your eyes now."

His command reaches right into my soul, and I obey without hesitation. That's what I desire so badly. To trust someone to take control and tell me what to do.

"Good boy," he murmurs.

Like—even that's perfect. I want to be his good boy now that the role play is over. But in the moment, being his good girl was the most incredible feeling I've ever experienced. And he just knows that.

I'm not walking away from this. Not without a fight.

"I'm sorry you regret what just happened," I say, managing to keep the tremor from my voice. "But that was the most incredible sex I ever had."

There. Cards on the table.

His face crumples. "Oh, no," he says, wrapping his arms around me and letting me nuzzle against his neck. "I don't regret you, sweet boy. You were incredible. Spectacular."

That goes some way to mollifying me.

"Then what's wrong?" I ask.

He tightens his hands around the soft blanket he covered me with. For modesty or warmth or both, I'm not sure. But it's the kind of attentive, thoughtful aftercare I crave. I've had some good experiences with Doms before when I've managed to find them. But mostly, I've just had hookups with disappointing men who clearly have alpha male issues. Getting kicked out of bed after rough sex isn't something I particularly enjoy.

So I snuggle against Benedict, absorbing all his warmth and tenderness. He's stroking his fingers against the short hairs at the base of my skull, making me shiver.

"I'm a *teacher*," he eventually utters.

Oh. *Oh.*

It all suddenly clicks into place. His meltdown just now. Why calling him 'Sir' has been such an issue.

I shake my head and lean back to look him in the eyes. "It was a role play," I insist. "A game between two consensual adults."

He also shakes his head, still looking stricken. "No one's ever... I've never... I've never played like that before with anyone who knows I'm actually a professor. Who knows me at all out of the scene. It just...*happened.*"

Whoa.

I know I shouldn't be thinking of myself right now, but holy fuck, I'm honored by that. Like, deeply, seriously proud. But this isn't about me. This is about reassuring my friend—my new lover—that everything is honestly fine.

Aftercare can go both ways.

I grip the back of his head and make him look at me where we're both kneeling on the floor. At least his rug is soft under our knees.

"It was a fantasy," I tell him clearly. "One I absolutely loved. It was fun between two consenting adults."

He's still shaking his head, though. "I didn't check

anything with you beforehand," he whispers. "Safe words, limits, nothing."

"Everyone knows how to use traffic lights," I say breezily.

Because, yeah. Technically I guess we should have stopped and talked some things through before going kind of hardcore on the slut shaming and all that. But this is real life, and sometimes there isn't the perfect moment for all that stuff.

"We can discuss it all now or before next time or whatever," I press on.

His eyes go wide. "Next time?"

I swallow, determined not to let a good thing slip through my fingers. "Yes, I want a next time," I say firmly. "I want to be your pretty schoolgirl again and feel your cock in my ass. I have *so* many more sets of lingerie, and no one's ever gotten to see them!"

My silly joke does help him to crack a smile, but he's still looking at me curiously. I can't help but feel like the panic is subsiding slightly, though. At least I hope it is.

"This is so wrong," he says, dashing my hopes. "I shouldn't want this. What if anyone found out? The whole student/teacher dynamic is unethical and depraved and—"

"Hey, hey," I say, gripping his shoulders. "No. Stop that. Have you ever had sex with an actual underage student?"

The look of pure horror that floods his face answers my question before he does. "No!" he cries, looking physically sick. "Absolutely not. No student ever. I've never even been attracted to anyone like that. No!"

I rub his arms and nod, giving him what I hope is a reassuring smile. "Exactly. Benedict, please listen to me. I don't want to try and explain your own kink to you, but you're a Dom, right?" He nods. "You like having good little subs at your feet, desperate to suck your cock."

He nods again, but this time he reaches up and caresses

the side of my face. I let out a small whimper and lean into the touch.

"*Pretty* little subs," he stresses, and I glow with pride.

"That's my kink," I whisper, still not quite able to believe I finally just enacted an actual scene to fulfill that need. I felt so fucking gorgeous and pretty and feminine it was unreal.

Benedict gives me a small but happy laugh. "I guessed," he says kindly. "Jackson, I know we're trying to sort through my shit right now, but I have to tell you how honored I am that I was the first man you ever let see your beautiful underwear. You are stunning, and I'm sorry you felt like you had to hide it."

I swallow. That lump of emotion is trying to crawl back up my throat again, but this time for a so much better reason. "Thank you," I whisper. "I-I was so afraid. I'm so happy I got to share it with you."

He leans forward and gives me a sweet kiss on the lips. "Good boy," he murmurs.

"Yes," is all I can say to try and convey that's what I want so badly. To be his good boy.

A good boy for Daddy.

That's a discussion for another time, though. I have no idea if that's a name he'd be into, and he's wobbly enough right now.

"You don't need to be afraid, either," I insist, bringing the conversation back to him.

He looks at me with those big brown eyes, and I know I'll do anything I can to make him feel better again. To be the impressive Dom who claimed me so thoroughly.

"What we did—me calling you 'Sir'—all of it. It was just power play," I continue. "I did a fully consensual scene once where I fought the whole time like I didn't want it. Some people wouldn't understand that. Because in real life, that kind of act is abhorrent. But I consented. I gave all my power over to that Dom to do whatever he wanted with me, and it was actually the safest, most freeing experience of my life. I had my safe words, but I didn't need them. And afterward, he held me and told me how well I did and how perfect I'd been for him. We both got an incredible time out of it. I've been wanting something like that again ever since."

I realize I've said a lot, so I press my lips together and watch Benedict for his reaction. He's still got his palm pressed reassuringly against my face, and he just looks at me for a few moments. I feel like I can see his clever mind working, and I wonder if anyone has ever tried to give him permission for enjoying his kinks or if he's hidden them away in shame for all this time.

The thought breaks my heart.

"You wanted to be dominated like that more?" he asks, and I nod.

Honestly, I can see where his very real fears stem from. But he's not doing anything wrong at all. In fact, I'm already salivating at the idea of what he could give me. What I could give him with my submission. How fulfilling we could be for each other.

"I want to see where this goes," I say earnestly. "And I know there are other concerns. We work together."

"Your godmother would kill me if she ever found out," he adds with a chuckle, and I have to agree.

"But you're leaving in four months," I remind him. "We have a window of opportunity to explore this exciting thing between us, but without any pressure. It can just be a fling. Something to remember Paddle Creek by."

He really laughs at that. "Like a magnet or a T-shirt?"

I nod proudly. "That reads 'I fucked Jackson Riggs into next week' on it." I waggle my eyebrows playfully at him, making him laugh even more.

He puffs out his cheeks and shakes his head. "It all sounds so reasonable when you talk about it like that."

I place my hand on his chest, feeling his heart beating. "That's because it is. It's two adults consenting to something that makes them feel so good. It's pleasure and satisfaction and wish fulfillment. It doesn't matter if other people might not understand it, because they'll never have to know about it."

He nods and takes a few steadying breaths before wrapping his arms around me again. "I'm the Dom," he grumbles. *"I'm* supposed to be taking care of *you."*

I scoff and rub his back. "Aftercare is for everyone who needs it. Besides, the first thing you did was snuggle me up in this blanket. And you told me I was good."

He shakes his head against mine. "I believe I said 'spectacular,' pretty boy."

I hum. "Okay, then. But if you feel like you want to do more, I'm kind of sticky. Maybe you could shower with me?"

He looks down at the cum getting a little gross on my stomach and chest. It's okay he forgot about it for a moment. He was having a pretty big crisis. But something in me really hopes we're past the worst of that now.

"I'd *love* to shower with you," he says, beaming with happiness and what I'm sure is relief. "Then perhaps we can cuddle for a while. Talk some more about what we want from this. And I want you to stay for dinner."

There we go. There's my sexy Dom back again. He should have just told me I'm staying for dinner, but we can work up to that. I'm sure he's more than capable.

My heart flutters, and I feel all gooey. "I'd love that, Sir," I say softly.

He kisses me on the mouth. "Thank you," he says. I don't ask for what. I feel the same way.

Thank you for letting me be me.

CHAPTER 10

Benedict

I AM FUCKING EXHAUSTED.

I guess this must be similar to sub drop. Doms also get highs and lows, after all. But I can't think that I've ever felt this kind of out-of-body tiredness before.

We're lying on my bed, and Jackson's hard, warm body is pressed against mine. His hair is damp, and he smells like my shower gel, which makes a primal part of me very happy.

I wondered if he expected something more sexual to happen when we were getting cleaned up, but he seemed perfectly happy to sway against me as I rinsed him thoroughly, washing away the physical evidence of our tryst.

The emotional ramifications are going to stick around a hell of a lot longer, but I'm okay with that. I'm thrilled, actually.

But there's also a *lot* rattling around in my head, and I'm grateful that he's all right with us simply being still and calm for now.

This man. He might be young, but he's certainly got some wisdom going on for his years. He's made me think about some things about myself and my kink in ways that truly had never occurred to me before.

Maybe I'm really not as fucked up as I feared.

I stroke his back and press an easy kiss to his temple. It's surprising how fast we've shifted the nature of our relationship. Those walls I'd so carefully built were smashed with just one swing of his hammer. I guess what we're feeling now —this incredibly strong pull between us—has been lurking since the moment we met. If I hadn't been so stubborn, I might have seen that a lot sooner.

He shifts against me. He's dressed once again in his jeans and hoodie, and I switched from shirt and trousers to jogging bottoms and a Henley. His lingerie got dirty, but he was happy to borrow a pair of my clean boxers for now.

In fact, he was extremely pleased by my offer. It does feel like quite a leap to lend him something of mine, but we're here now, and I'm not walking it back. I love to think of my underwear hugging his most intimate areas as we snuggle up together. It's cozy and domestic. Dotty is even curled up at our feet.

"Are you okay?" Jackson asks me. He's checked that a couple of times now, but I don't mind.

I almost fucked this up completely.

Honestly, it's my job as the Dom to make sure my sub is taken care of. The way I behaved could have seriously damaged him. I'm very thankful that he's a lot more emotionally mature than I gave him credit for.

"I'm shaken," I tell him sincerely. "I think I might even be in a form of mild shock. But also…I'm kind of amazing."

He grins at that and wiggles closer to me—if that's possible. "I'm really glad to hear that, Benedict."

I love the way he says my name. There's a possessiveness to it.

I think about my options.

He was right in what he said earlier. I only have four months left here in town. Maybe five depending on when I book my flights. That feels like a safe amount of time to commit to something fun but without the pressure of how it would actually function in the real world. It could be our naughty little secret.

Although I must admit that even though I *know* the reasons it's kind of taboo, it's not feeling like something to be ashamed of in this moment, which is astonishing to me. I thought I was having a nervous breakdown in the aftermath of realizing what I'd done. But the way Jackson talked about my kinks made them seem so…okay.

I'm not stupid. Logically, I understand that it's consensual power play. But the shame that's been building in me for so many years has definitely warped my brain. I'm still very uneasy about the idea of mixing work and kink in any way, but Jackson seems so positive and confident that it won't be a problem.

I can't deny that what we shared this afternoon was explosive and intoxicating, and even though I still have my worries and doubts, it would be very hard to walk away from this now.

Time to start acting like the Dom I know I am again, then.

"Jackson," I say. "What do you want from this? What do you see happening?"

He shifts and looks up at me with his big blue eyes. He's calm rather than anxious, and I love that energy about him.

"You're leaving in May, right?"

"Or June," I confirm. "I'm not sure how long it'll take to tie up all my loose ends, but I'll want to see this last class graduate."

He nods. "Then…what I want is something like this. I want to keep seeing each other for scenes or play sessions. If that's all you want, that's okay. But I'd also like to just see you for you. Like, how you said about staying for dinner tonight. I'd love that. But…I think it would be best if we kept everything private. It's nobody's else's business. So I wouldn't expect you to take me out anywhere super public or hold my hand or treat me differently at work." He licks his lips, the first hint of nervousness flickering across his face. "How does that sound?"

I study him for a moment, caressing his neck. "I think that sounds like a dream," I admit. "And will you wear your pretty lingerie for me?"

He beams like he can't believe what I've just asked. "Every day!" he cries sweetly. "I might even be able to justify buying some new stuff." He waggles his eyebrows, making me laugh.

"Is that so, naughty boy?"

He bites his lip and looks up at me shyly through his long lashes. "There's something else as well," he says, sounding a lot less confident than when he launched into his previous proposition.

I raise my eyebrows at him. "Of course."

"*Can* I be your boy? Or sometimes your girl, like in the scene?"

I'd almost forgotten about that in all the panic that ensued. I can't help but exhale and give him a small smile. "I got that right, then?"

Jackson shakes his head. "You got it *perfect.* I've never quite scened like that before. Not in full role play. And being your good little slutty girl was hot as fuck."

I kiss him on his lips, feeling something stir in me again. "You were so perfect," I murmur against his lips. "I've never had a good girl kneel for me before. I loved it."

He blinks at me. "Really? It didn't, um, make you feel any less gay?"

I laugh. "Absolutely not," I say easily, and rub his back. "It might not be obvious from the epic meltdown, but I'm very confident in my attractions to people. I use the label 'gay,' but I don't really care what's between a person's legs, their pronouns, or gender identity." I brush our noses together. "Although I will confess that seeing your big cock in that dainty underwear was sinfully delicious."

He squirms against me, but I just hold him tighter. "Oh, wow. Okay, then," he says bashfully.

"So shall we make that a rule?" I suggest, happy to be discussing terms in more depth. "You're my good boy unless we do a scene, then you're my good girl?"

He thinks a minute, then nods. "Yes, if I'm playing a character. If we just have more vanilla sex, I'd like to be your boy then as well."

I nod, thinking this might need a bit of testing out, but I'm happy enough to feel our way through. "Your pronouns are he, him, his?" I check and he nods again.

"Yes," he tells me. "I've thought about this. I wondered if I might be trans for a while. I think I'm not completely cis—you know, identifying totally with the gender I was assigned at birth. But I'm not a trans woman. I love my body as it is, and I'm a man. I just really love feeling feminine at certain times. I guess maybe like a lot of drag queens do?"

I nod again. "That makes sense to me," I say.

He nibbles his lip for a minute, thinking. "I've kept this secret for so long, it's funny to be talking about it with anyone else. Aside from Selena, of course. But she's just so fiercely adamant that I need to be myself. It's different talking about it with…"

"Someone you just shared orgasms with?" I suggest.

He laughs. "Yeah, that. Thank you."

"You're very welcome," I assure him with another kiss.

"And you?" he asks.

I frown. "What about me?" I reply with a warm curiosity.

He smiles. "I know you like being called 'Sir,'" he says slyly.

"Oh," I say with a nod and a grin. "Yes, I do. Anything like that turns me on. Sir. Master. I even had a sub call me 'My Lord' for a while." He chuckles, but there's something in his eyes that's giving me pause. "Do those not work for you?"

He quickly shakes his head. "In scenes, yeah. Absolutely. Seriously hot. Happy to play with anything like that."

"But?"

"But every day as well?" he checks.

I also chuckle. "No, that's fine. You can call me Benedict or a pet name if you like."

He swallows and looks even more nervous than when he asked about being my boy or the lingerie. "Daddy?" he suggests.

I feel my eyebrows rise. So, I was right about that earlier. Still, it's a bit of a surprise to have it confirmed.

"That's a new one for me," I admit. But then I look at him, so sweet and lovely in my arms, my good, pretty boy, and something about it makes sense. "So you want to keep some of the kink going out of scenes," I say. It's not a question because it's already quite clear to me. "You want Daddy to take care of you."

He drops his gaze, his face going adorably red. "I've wanted a Daddy for a while now, and I think you'd be really good at it. You like taking care of people. Like coming and picking me up in your car. I loved that. I thought maybe we could try it out. But if it's weird for you—"

"No, no," I say quickly. "The name is new, but you're right. I get a lot out of taking care of my partners outside of sex. How much responsibility would you want to try giving me?" I can't see him wanting to give up *all* of his own decision-making.

He considers a minute. "Just…a little. Like today. I liked

when you put the blanket on me, and I'm looking forward to dinner. I'd enjoy helping if you wanted or needed me to chop veggies or something, but I wouldn't mind a bit of doting if you just wanted to make it. Only if you'd enjoy that," he adds. "I don't want to be greedy."

It's my turn to shake my head. "You wouldn't be. I like the idea of a little pampering and spoiling for my good boy. So if we're talking love languages, that sounds like acts of service to me."

We had a conversation about love languages in relation to a class I taught last semester, so I know he knows what I'm talking about. Sure enough, he nods and doesn't look confused or like he needs me to explain about the five different branches.

"How about gift-giving?" I ask. "Words of affirmation? Quality time and physical touch seem like a given."

We both laugh, and I'm loving the rosy glow on his cheeks. He's still a bit embarrassed but he's asking for what he wants and needs.

Good boy.

"Definitely words," he tells me. "Everything you said in the scene was magical. And out of it, now. Like calling me your good boy and pretty and all that." He frowns. "I'm not really into gifts. Not expensive things or anything, I mean. I love stuff that's thoughtful. Last Christmas Selena got me a scented candle from one of those places that sell girly pajamas. It's called Slumber Party and smells like strawberries and cream. It didn't cost much, but I light it all the time because it makes me feel super feminine, and she knew that it would. I love it so much."

"Duly noted," I say.

"Thank you, Daddy," he replies quietly.

I let it settle over me. It's a much softer vibe than I usually go for, but then I haven't let kink spill out into my life for several years now, not since I was back in Oxford and then some. Maybe I've gotten older and changed. I like the idea of being Jackson's Daddy. At the very least, we can try it out. This limited window of time is really making me braver to experiment in ways I usually wouldn't dare.

"You're welcome, good boy," I say, and he beams, snuggling against me. "So, what do you want now? It's a bit early for dinner, but I could also make you a light lunch. Or we could watch TV, play a game, give Dotty another w-a-l-k." I spell it out so she doesn't start going mental, but she still lifts her head and gives me a curious look before going back to sleep.

"How about more cuddles and kisses with Daddy?" Jackson asks coyly, but there's a hint of brattishness there that stirs me.

"Just cuddles and kisses?" I say with an arched eyebrow, already pulling him farther down the bed so we're lying side-by-side. I kiss his neck and make him moan. A thump on the floor tells me that Dotty has taken that as her cue to skedaddle, which is lucky because Jackson is already grinding against me. "I think good boys might deserve more than just that."

"Yes, Daddy," he says breathlessly, clinging to me, his eyes shining brightly. "You can do anything you want with me. I'm your good boy."

Urgh. "Anything?" I repeat, already getting hard again.

He nods, dragging his lower lip through his teeth slowly. "Yes, Sir," he purrs.

"Good boy," I tell him before capturing his mouth for a filthy kiss.

We can talk more about his interests over dinner. Spanking, bondage, humiliation, voyeurism, exhibitionism. I have a long list. Right now, calling him pretty and swapping blow jobs seems like a very safe and utterly delightful option.

I have a sub—a boy.

At least for the next few months.

CHAPTER 11

Jackson

"Whoa, there!" I cry as I'm walking around the corner of the hallway away from Benedict's office. "Where's the fire?"

A young man I don't recognize bounces off me and looks stricken. "Sorry!" he squeaks, swiping the mop of dark hair out of his eyes. "I was hoping to catch Professor Knight before he left for the day. I'm confused about an assignment." He shakes his head and clenches his fists. "Sorry. I'm one of his masters students. He teaches classics."

I laugh gently. This poor dude is strung out to within an inch of his life. "I know. I'm his TA," I tell him kindly. "Anything I can help you with? Admin-wise, I mean," I amend. "If it's anything in Latin, I've got nothing for you except enthusiasm and a few months on Duolingo."

That gets a small laugh out of him, which makes me happy. I know students take their studies seriously, but I hate seeing them lose their minds over stuff that really won't matter in a few years' time.

"Oh, thanks," he says bashfully. "But it's probably best I talk to the professor myself. I'm, um, really new here. I transferred at the start of this semester from Albertson. He doesn't know me that well yet, and I have a few different questions."

That's unusual to switch up in the middle of the year. I wonder what this kid's story is.

Kid. I have to laugh at myself. He's probably only a couple of years younger than me.

"Have you emailed him?" The guy shakes his head, but that just makes me smile. I know the answer to this because I know Benedict so well now. "My advice would always be to email him. Be-Professor Knight isn't in his office all that often, and he hates feeling like he didn't give his students enough feedback. So long as you don't mind waiting a few hours, he'll answer all your questions and then some in an email. Do you have the address?"

"Uh, maybe?" the guy says.

"No worries," I tell him. "Let me write it down for you now."

I expect him to hand his phone over, but instead, he gets out a brand-new-looking hardback notebook, flips to a page, then hands it over to me. The title reads "Useful Information" and has several other emails, phone numbers, dates, times, and such written down. I quickly scribble Benedict's details for him, then hand it back.

"What's your name?" I ask before he can run off like I'm sure he's going to. "So I can mention you to the professor and make sure he replies to your email first."

The kid—I can't help it, he seems *so* young to be doing a masters—gives me a relieved smile. "Xander," he tells me. "Alexander Patterson. Thank you. I'd really appreciate that."

"Jackson Riggs," I say, jerking my thumb at my chest. "Nice to meet you."

The kid gives an awkward laugh, like that couldn't

possibly be true. "Well, um, bye," he says before rushing back the way he came.

Since I'm also going in that direction, I wait a few minutes, playing with my phone. I don't want him to feel like he's being followed, although I am a little worried about him. I console myself that Benedict will look after him.

He's very good at looking after people. I'm learning just how true that is firsthand.

I shiver and reread his latest message back for the hundredth time.

BENEDICT: Let yourself in. I expect to find you in your pretties lying upside down on my bed. Stretch yourself. I know you'll be a good boy for Daddy.

It's been a week since our relationship imploded and changed entirely for the better. We haven't really had the chance to connect much beyond a few make-out sessions in his locked office, but that's just meant the anticipation has been building.

I've worn different lingerie for him every day and made sure he knew it, whether that was inviting him to feel me up or sending him photos. It's been exhilarating. I'd spent so long worrying what might happen if I told a guy my secret I never really stopped to consider how *amazing* it could also be.

I've enjoyed teasing Benedict with it, showing him what lies in store for him the next time he can get me alone. I think we've both really gotten off knowing that it's still a secret from everyone else. I kind of felt like that sometimes before, but sharing the knowledge with Benedict just makes it all that more tantalizing. And knowing I'm driving him wild is intoxicatingly powerful.

All things considered, I think we've both been pretty patient. But now the week is done. It's Friday night, and I'm so very ready to be fucked all the way into Monday.

Yesterday, he gave me a key, which I thought I kept extremely cool about in the moment. Naturally, I screamed at Selena the moment I got her on the phone. She's heard everything I can tell her about the situation without betraying Benedict's privacy, but she's fully supportive of what we're doing. She'd have made a #TEAM BENESON T-shirt if I'd let her.

Along with the key, Benedict told me to pack a weekend bag and not skimp on the lingerie. I've probably crammed enough clothes, toiletries, and so on into my gym bag for a full week's vacation. Not to mention lube, condoms, my favorite dildo, the soft restraints I've never gotten to use with anyone else yet, and my toothbrush.

I want to have minty fresh breath after all the cock I plan on sucking.

Seriously, how have all my wildest fantasies come true? Every morning I've woken up and had to pinch myself as all the memories come flooding back to me. I'm the luckiest boy who's sometimes a girl in the whole world.

I guess the trade-off is that this is temporary, and that's okay. Benedict could have returned back to England without either of us admitting how we felt, and we'd have missed out on so much. Being temporary makes it safer in some ways because it's more freeing for us to try stuff out.

I still can't actually believe I had the guts to ask if I could call him 'Daddy' after showing him my underwear as well. Talk about getting my cake and eating it.

Speaking of cake, I decided to get ahead of the game and stretch myself out in the bathroom about an hour ago. I'm wearing my favorite plug to keep me ready for my Daddy (or Sir, technically). Now that the coast is clear, I head out to my car in the parking lot, feeling little jolts of pleasure with each movement.

As I walk down the path away from the humanities building, I see a flash of brown-and-white fur dash behind a low wall. I pause and watch, then a pair of dark eyes peer over the bricks, checking the coast is clear.

Clayton, the campus's unofficial mascot. I know technically raccoons are pests, but I think he's adorable, and I know I'm not the only one. He seems to think he's safe enough because from behind the low wall, he lifts a soda can that looks huge in his tiny paws, tips it up, then splashes what's left of the cola over his face, probably only drinking about a third of the bubbly liquid. But then he throws the can over the wall and starts cleaning his sticky fur quite happily.

"Litter bug," I say with a shake of my head. I guess the noise and movement are enough to alert him of my presence. His fuzzy little head snaps around. He sees me and predictably flees, his bushy tail vanishing behind the wall. But that leaves me free to walk over, pick up the can, and toss it in the recycling.

Ahh, Paddle Creek. Never change.

As I sit in my banged-up car and wait for the heater to thaw it out, I twist the rearview mirror and look at myself for a minute.

I'm sure I wasn't completely overthinking the lingerie thing. I had people treat me like dirt online and had threats in real life from the mere idea of something feminine like that. I wasn't imagining things.

However, Selena was right. I just needed to find the right man to accept me. And I can't wait to show him everything I have tucked away in my bag right now.

But what I didn't expect was to be called a girl and fucking love it. I meant what I said. I'm sure it only applies to scenes. But hearing Benedict call me 'good girl' and 'pretty girl' and whatever else, gave me life in ways I'd never imagined before.

I study my reflection and run my thumb against the dark

stubble on my chin. I don't *look* like a pretty girl. I've come to realize in this past week that I've definitely got a disconnect in my head between how I look and how I feel…or I guess, not what I feel. But what I feel is all right to expect from people.

I never thought I'd be made to feel as beautiful as I have by Benedict in such a short time. It's got me wondering what else I want.

Nothing surgical. I meant what I said. I love my body. I work out hard and look fucking hot. I love the hard ridges and planes, the hair, the smell, everything.

But what if I could add other pretty things to it?

I turn my head this way and that, thinking about my eyes. What would they look like with a little eyeliner? Some glitter? I've seen some great tutorials where guys just use foundation and basic contouring as well as filling in their eyebrows, and they look like walking Instagram filters. If women can do it, why can't men? I think I might give it a go.

And I try and suppress a little shiver, telling myself it doesn't matter what Daddy might have to say about it. But I can't help but longingly imagine that he'll call me gorgeous and perfect. I'd be doing it for myself. However, it wouldn't hurt if Benedict approved as well.

I want to be pretty for him.

My car seems to finally be warm enough to agree to cooperate, so I check my mirrors and reverse out of the parking bay. It's a short drive to Benedict's. Everywhere in Paddle Creek is a short drive, realistically. But I have to be careful not to speed anyway. I'm just so eager to get there and be ravaged by Sir again I'm practically salivating.

I notice when I park up that his Prius isn't there. He mentioned when he left work before me that he was going to get a quick walk in for Dotty, and sure enough, when I let myself through the door, I'm not greeted by any raucous barking.

My nerves jangle as I head to his bedroom and quickly undress down to my lingerie, folding my clothes neatly on top of the dresser. Today's ensemble is flamingo pink, but I have a different kind of panties on today. These are my favorite style, with a peek-a-boo hole in the back so I don't have to take them off as I ease the plug out in Benedict's en suite and wash it.

I'm really hoping today is the day he fucks my ass, and I want to keep all my gorgeous satin and lace on for him while he does.

I touch my cock and bite my lip as I look at my reflection for the second time in as many minutes. Yeah. I love myself like this. I look ridiculously hot. And now I'm going to lie in wait for my Daddy to come home.

My heart is thumping as I do as he asked and lie down with my head at the foot of the bed. I stretch my arms out and take deep breaths as I look at the ceiling. I'm anxious how long I'm going to have to wait, but then I realize that's out of my hands. I don't have to worry about it. My only job was to get here. Daddy will decide all the rest. So I start to kind of float as I focus on the white paint above me, drifting into a sleepy trance.

I'm not sure how long I lie there before I hear keys jangle and the door opening accompanied by Dotty's barking. "Shh, that's it, good girl," Benedict's voice rumbles through the apartment. "Go and lie down now, good girl."

The barking stops, and I wonder if Benedict's given her one of the chew sticks she loves. That'll keep her distracted for a while. My toes curl. I'm certainly hoping to distract Benedict for most of the evening.

Most of the weekend.

God, I can't believe I went so many months without sex

before this. Now I'm desperate, like a horny teenager who's just discovered jerking off.

It's *so* much better when someone else is making the orgasm happen, though.

"There you are," Benedict rasps harshly. Even though I've been straining to hear him for the past several minutes, his appearance still makes me jump. I shiver and bite my lip. I can sort of see him from the corner of my eye, but he soon slips from my line of sight, and a jolt of primal fear runs through me.

It's delicious.

"I've been waiting for you, Sir," I say breathlessly.

"Of course you have, you little slut." He's somewhere behind me now. I could try and twist around to see him, but that's not the point. I'm at his mercy, and that's the way I like it. "I suppose you think this is going to impress me?"

I'm quivering now. My mouth is dry, and my cock is throbbing against the silky satin that encases it.

"I'm sorry, Sir," I whimper. "I just really need that recommendation letter. My whole law career depends on it!"

Law? If I weren't so into the scene already, I'd definitely laugh at myself. I'm not sure where that came from. I've probably watched too many TV shows. But it's kind of hot and different from the grades thing we did last time.

"You should have thought about that before you slacked off in so many of my classes," Benedict growls. "Too busy jumping on every cock you see. Well, now it's my turn."

He suddenly looms over me. He's still got most of his clothes on—navy pants and light blue shirt, a silver-striped tie loosened around his collar. But he's holding his dick which is sticking out of his zipper, and he roughly rubs the tip against my mouth.

"If I let you fuck me, will you write the letter?" I ask.

He grabs my hair with his free hand, tugging my head

back and sliding his length against my tongue. "It depends on how well you take my cock, slut," he says, slapping it against my lips and chin.

Being upside down is disorienting, but that adds to the rush of it all. He lunges out and grabs my wrists, hauling them up and smacking my hands against his ass. Then he seizes his cock again and thrusts it down my throat.

"That's it, good girl. Take it all. Choke on it." He fucks my mouth as I slurp him down. It's hard to keep my eyes open, but I manage it, not wanting to miss a single moment of him dominating me. He leans over me, making me hold his dick in place as he reaches down and starts massaging my chest through the bra. "Such gorgeous tits. I bet you use these to get whatever you want."

He pinches both my nipples hard through the material, making me moan around his cock. I'm struggling to breathe through my nose and am feeling dizzy. The lightheadedness is glorious, though. I'm really floating now, my whole world reduced to the way Benedict's body parts feel against me.

We haven't discussed breath play, though, so I'm not really surprised when Benedict pulls out and lets me gasp for air. I'm not sure I'd actually want much more than he gave me. Besides, I want to keep playing the game, and that means talking.

"No, Sir," I protest. "I'm a good girl. I'd *never* use my body to get something I wanted."

"Liar," he snarls. "Everyone knows you use that pussy to open whatever door you need. Now I'm going to see what all the fuss is about. Get on your knees."

I scramble around on the bed until I'm kneeling up and facing him. The sudden shift must drop my blood pressure, because I sway quite violently. But Benedict is there, grabbing my shoulders with firm hands and steadying me on the bed before him. Then he seizes my chin and kisses my mouth hungrily. My body sings at the way he's taking control of it.

"I *am* a slut," I murmur against his lips, squeezing his ass. "I'm ready for you, Sir. I've been waiting for you to come and fill my pussy up with your big cock. Please fuck me. *Please.*"

He grunts and bites my lower lip. "I knew it," he whispers. "You're desperate for it. Such a needy little girl." He caresses my cock through my underwear as he says that, making me cry out. "Oh, yes. So hard for Sir. But you don't get to come until I say so, understand?"

I nod frantically. He slips his hand around, stroking my bare ass cheek before sliding his fingers down my crack and probing my stretched-out hole.

"Oh, you *are* ready for me," he says in delight. "Naughty girl."

He removes his hand and gives my butt a sharp slap, making me gasp and swoon against him, the endorphins racing through me.

He grins, then runs both his hands up and down my body, feeling the lingerie against my skin. "So pretty," he says, capturing my lips for another kiss. "So good for Sir." He wraps his hand around my neck. "Perhaps I should get you a collar so I can drag you around wherever I want you. For now…"

He lets me go and loosens his tie further, but still keeps the knot intact. He lifts it over his head, then slips it over mine, giving it a tug to tighten it again. It's still quite open where it rests on my collarbones, but the rush it's giving me is incredible. I'm not only wearing something of his, but he pulls at it, encouraging me to drop to all fours on the mattress and turn around.

He keeps a hold of it as he walks around the bed, his shiny red cock still proudly sticking out of his pants. He only lets go of the tie to rearrange himself so his trousers and briefs are pushed down to his thighs. Then he sits on the bed with his back against the pillows and his legs stretched out between my limbs. I wait for him to lead me with the tie before I crawl over to him and straddle his hips.

Wordlessly, he reaches over and opens the drawer next to him just enough to fish out the condom and bottle of lube that he must have stashed there, ready and waiting. I lick my lips and repress a moan, thinking of how hot that is. He's *ready* to fuck me. Perhaps he has been all week.

He crooks his fingers, calling me down to kiss him as he quickly slides the rubber on. I cling to his shirt and grind my hard length against his stomach. He doesn't warn me as he pushes a slippery, lube-covered finger inside my hole, slicking me up and making me cry out.

"Be a good girl now and fuck Sir's brains out, hmm? Show me why I should help get a little slut like you into law school. If I held you back a year, I could keep you here and fuck you whenever I wanted."

I moan loudly, impaling myself on his hot, hard shaft. "Please, Sir," I beg, looking deep into his eyes. "I'll be good. I'll do anything."

His expression is one of savage hunger as I force his length inside me. "I know you will, pretty girl. So good for Sir. You're at my mercy. *I'll* decide if you're good enough. Give me a show. Ride me hard."

I grunt, tears in my eyes as he bottoms out, filling me to the brim. "Your cock feels fucking amazing," I rasp, and he grins.

"I know."

He grabs the back of my head and kisses me roughly as I start rocking my hips. His tip hits my prostate with every thrust, making me wail into his mouth.

"That's it, good girl," he growls. "Take it all. Take it hard. Tell me you love it."

"I love it, Sir," I sob. "It feels so good."

He rubs my pecs and pinches my already erect nipples. He snaps the garter straps against my thighs and spanks my ass again, each little flash of pain flying straight to my balls and making me cry out in pleasure.

"Good girl," he murmurs into my mouth. "That's it, just like that. So good for Sir. So obedient and pretty."

"Please, Sir, please," I beg as I bounce frantically on his cock, slowing down and squeezing my hole around it. "Come in me. Tell me I'm special."

"The only thing you're good for, slut, is fucking," he snarls. "It's a good thing you look fucking spectacular with my dick sliding in and out of your wet pussy. I'm going to fuck you whenever I feel like it. Just bend you over my desk and take you, and you're going to love it."

"I will, I will," I wail, dropping my head back. He runs his hand up the tie, wrapping it tighter around his hand before squeezing my neck. *"Sir,"* I moan, feeling the word vibrate through my throat against his palm.

He jerks his hips, snapping them up to meet my downward thrusts. I feel like he's trying to split me in two, and I gasp and cry, digging my fingers into his shoulders. His breathing is ragged, and I think he's getting close. I pick up the pace, fucking him as hard and fast as I can while I bite my lip and stare at him through my lashes.

"Come inside me, Sir," I whisper.

He throws his arms around my back, hauling me against him as he starts to shake and gnash his teeth. Even through the condom, I can feel his cock pulsing as he climaxes. Then he's kissing the shit out of me, reaching between us to free my cock from my panties and jerking me off frantically. I whimper and grip onto his shirt again, chasing the high.

It doesn't take long. I was already so turned on that all he really had to do was put his hands on me. Within seconds, I'm shouting and coming all over his shirt.

"Good boy," Benedict murmurs, rubbing my back as I ride out the last shockwaves. Then I collapse against his chest, where he continues rubbing my back and up my neck, kissing my temple and cheek. "Such a good boy for Daddy."

I'm not sure if the noise that escapes my throat is a laugh or a cry, but I cling to him and lap up all his praise. "Thank you, Daddy," I utter. That's all I want, is to be good for him.

Don't get me wrong, that was epic. And unlike last time, no freak-out follows. However…call me crazy, but I feel like Benedict might still be holding back a little. I know this is his kink and he initiated the role play, but…I don't know. Something is gnawing at me. Maybe it's in the way we cling to each other as our bodies cool and the highs fade. Yeah, there's definitely something lingering there that's still unsure.

I think there's something more I could be doing for him. Something different. He needs to know that this power play is fucking hot, and I'm so into it.

A plan starts to form.

Oh. Oh, yeah.

This is going to be fun.

CHAPTER 12

Benedict

I WAS SLIGHTLY SKEPTICAL ABOUT GIVING JACKSON A KEY SO soon into our relationship, but after walking in on him for that first planned scene, any doubts I had flew out of the window. It turns out that having a willing sex slave waiting for me when I get home is *definitely* part of my kink.

But it's more than that. This flat has felt so empty the whole time I've lived in it, even with Dotty and her larger-than-life personality. Jackson might not have moved any possessions in or anything, but his energy is already permeating the walls. The place feels warmer, and I've loved seeing his shoes at the door and his toothbrush in the mug next to mine.

I was worried it might get suffocating fast. I've never tried a kink lifestyle outside of the bedroom, and although I understand that Jackson wants me to look after him, I was worried what that might look like.

It turns out—so far at least—all I have to do is trust my instincts. He likes showering together, so we often do that after sex, and I get to wash him. I think that's the key—I *get* to wash him. It's a privilege. Like cooking him dinner and running his clothes through my machine. I like that he smells of my detergent now.

But it's not all one way. He snuck out this morning and made me breakfast in bed. It was just toast and sliced fruit and tea, but I swear I almost cried. No one's ever done anything for me like that, except maybe my mother when I was little and sick. He looked so bloody pleased with himself it was adorable.

I like him in my home. My dog likes him. I caught him wearing one of my hoodies, and it did something funny to my insides. I absolutely loved seeing my tie around his neck while we fucked.

Part of me is screaming that this is all happening too fast. But the reasonable part of me asks what is. What's too fast? We're only going to have a few months together. Why not jump in with both feet?

Besides, that part where I was worried about it being suffocating? Not an issue. Yeah, sure, we spent pretty much all of Friday night and Saturday fucking, but this morning he said he wanted to get a workout in at the gym while I graded some papers. Then he stayed in and organized those papers while I went on a quick grocery store run. I'd meant to stock up during the week but hadn't, and I imagine he has an impressive appetite most of the time, let alone when he's burning calories riding my cock twenty-four seven.

I grin as I let myself back into the apartment, thinking about how we'd shagged after he'd returned from the gym. I couldn't help it. He smelled so masculine and was glowing from the exercise. I practically jumped on him. We didn't even really scene, but he did call me Daddy, and I told him he was my good boy as I fucked him from behind on his hands and knees.

God, when was the last time my sex drive was this active? I've been so deprived thanks to a lack of scene around these parts, and I haven't prioritized hookups at all. Nope, it's just been my hand, my toys, and my healthy porn collection for a long while. Even so, that was only once, maybe twice a week. I'm not a young man anymore. I'm slightly worried about keeping up with Jackson's stamina. I usually run on Sunday mornings, but I might have to try and squeeze a couple more in, not to mention getting back to the gym.

That's something I can think about later. Right now, we just have one more evening left, and then it's back to work and pretending like nothing's going on until we get behind closed doors. I intend to savor these last few hours and hug him tightly through the night.

Dotty greets me at the door, wagging her tail happily. There's no sign of Jackson, and my bedroom door is closed. He might be napping, so I come in quietly with my bags and put everything away as efficiently as I can, planning on slipping into bed with my boy and snuggling until he wakes up.

Bless Dotty, she's so good. She understands something is going on, so when I give her one of her chew sticks, she obediently trots off with it to munch in the living room when she'll probably fall asleep. I wash my hands and fold away my reusable shopping bags, then creep over to creak open my bedroom door.

I freeze.

Jackson is not asleep.

Far from it.

He's wearing some sort of white toga—the costume kind students wear to frat house parties all the time. But he's also got gold glitter on his eyelids, and pink gloss shines on his lips. I think he's even wearing eyeliner. He's so fucking beautiful my heart flips. He's even got a tacky gold laurel on his head, and where the toga drapes open, I think I can see white lingerie with gold lace. Did he bring all that with him? Or did he grab it from his room after going to the gym? I'm guessing it's something he already had to hand and he's pulled it out just for us.

As delectable as that tableau is, that's not actually what's stopped my heart.

He's hooked a pair of soft cuffs through the slatted headboard that I bought specifically to attach fun things to but never have. His wrists are crossed above his head inside the bracelets. I note that he's hardly closed them at all so he could easily pull free if he needed to, but that's just for safety. The way he's waiting like that speaks crystal clear to me.

He's trapped. He's my prisoner. Waiting for me to return and have my wicked way with him.

"Sir," he cries as soon as he sees me, squirming divinely, acting like he can't break free. "Good Sir! I implore you to release me. My father—the king—won't stand for you kidnapping me. There could be war!"

Lust shoots through me from head to toe, landing firmly in my tingling balls. My cock throbs in my jeans, and my mouth waters. There are many things I'm starting to really appreciate about my boy now that our relationship has changed, but I can't deny how insanely hot it is that he's actually a pretty good actor. It looks like there's real fear in his wide eyes, and he struggles again as if he couldn't pull free from the restraints in a second.

For the briefest moment, that thought crosses my mind once more, and I wonder if there's something wrong and sadistic about me that I get off so hard on this kind of scenario. But…this isn't a naughty, slutty student.

This is a princess from a faraway land. This is all completely imaginary…and consensual. Jackson is giving me permission to do this.

"War?" I repeat, closing the door behind me and arching my eyebrow. "Is that so?"

He nods earnestly. "You might be the most renowned

scholar in all the land, but you'll never have the throne!" He drops his eyes and swallows. "Unless…unless you impregnate me with an heir. Is that your dastardly plan?"

Fuck. *Fuck.* Where did this man come from? I've done so many scenes, but it's never gotten…literary…before. Subs in clubs are generally naked or nearly so, and just up for something quick and dirty. Student and pupil has always been my go-to. I guess I've done boss and employee as well, where the sub begged me for a pay rise. But this is…creative.

I keep my eyes glued on Jackson as I hastily rip open the buttons on my shirt, grateful that I wore one to the store. Then I shove down my jeans and underwear, leaving me just in the open button-down. There. That's sort of a costume. Usually, I like to stay in almost all my clothes to assert a certain kind of dominance. But I like the idea of getting into character a lot right now.

"Oh, sweet, simple girl," I sneer as I march up the bed toward the restraints. I tighten the cuffs and fucking love the little, desperate gasp that escapes Jackson's mouth. That's right, pretty boy. You're mine now. "I have so many plans for you. But I wouldn't have dragged you here if I knew you didn't want it. Didn't *crave* it. I've seen you at the banquets and balls. You know you shouldn't want me, but you can't help it. You know I can set you *free.*"

"You brute!" Jackson cries, really pulling at the handcuffs now. Desire and domination play tug-of-war within me. "I'm a *good* girl! I would never want a cruel savage like you, no matter how handsome you are. You're clearly still a barbarian! When my father finds out—"

I lunge forward and grab his jaw, making him look at me. "He'll never find out until I announce that you're my bride and you're round with my child. Then *he'll* have to bend the knee to *me!*"

Jackson spits in my face. *"Never!"* he shouts.

Whoa.

I wasn't expecting that.

I wipe my face, then grab his throat, my chest heaving and my blood pumping. "You'll see, silly girl. You'll learn to love my cock. You'll worship it. And I've wasted enough time with your pathetic pleas. Now, this scholar is going to teach you how to be my loving slave."

I grab his hips and twist him. It sends the toga flying, but he doesn't actually resist, going obediently onto his knees. I look at how his arms are tied above his head, and run my hand gently between his shoulder blades.

"How does that feel, princess?" I ask gently.

"Like I'm about to get ravaged by a wicked, ungodly man!" he cries out, pulling theatrically at the handcuffs. "My father will send his armies. You'll see!"

Green, then. On we go.

I fling the rest of Jackson's skirts up to reveal his tight arse, cupped so beautifully by a full pair of beautiful white satin and gold lace knickers. They've got that exquisite oval-shaped gap in them, exposing his hole like the other pairs he's let me fuck him in all this weekend.

I run my hand reverently over the swell of his cheeks, then land a hard smack, making his arse jiggle perfectly. We talked about it, and he's not really into spanking for its own sake, but he said he loves a bit of it during sex, which is perfectly fine with me. I find the repetition of a full spanking session a little boring. But the yelp it elicits mid-scene is delicious.

I pull his cheeks apart and lick up his crack, earning a deep, throaty moan. "Who do you belong to?" I growl. "Who is your master? Who do you serve?"

"No one!" he cries. "Not you! Release me at once! I don't want you. I…I *can't* want you."

There it is. That thing that drives me wild. This princess

can protest all she wants, but *secretly* she's desperate for me.

I'm not sure anyone's understood my kink so well before Jackson. Perhaps not even myself.

"You *do* want me, and you're going to let me take you, princess," I say as I march over to my drawer to fetch lube and a condom. "You think you're all high and mighty, but deep down, you're nothing but a common wench. I see it, plain as day. No amount of sparkling crown jewels can distract from the fact that you're a needy little slut, and you're soon going to be screaming my name."

"Good Sir!" he shouts, scandalized. "You disgust me! I will never submit willingly to you!"

I shove a finger inside his arse, unsurprised to find him already stretched. "Then we shall have to start unwillingly, won't we?"

I don't waste any time in suiting up. He's stretched enough and this scene is not about making him comfortable. It's about me taking all the control and giving him what I know he needs.

I push past the ring of muscle, feeling his hole so tight and hot around me, even through the condom. "You brute! You monster!" he wails, yanking at the restraints but shoving his arse against my cock nonetheless. "My father—!"

I seize his hair and yank his head back, snarling in his ear. "Your father can come here, and I'll fuck him as well."

He moans wantonly. I'm worried about the pressure the cuffs are putting on him in that position, so I decide this is going to be hard and fast. I'm not sure how I'm going to make him come yet, but I can think clearly once I've orgasmed. I think I want to tease him, though. Make it slow and exquisite.

For now, I grab his hips and start to piston. "You're mine, princess," I bite out between thrusts. "Accept it. Worship me. I'm your king now. I'm going to fill you with my seed. I'm going to fuck you and *fuck* you until you are with my child, and then *no one* can take the kingdom from me!"

"Oh god, Sir, please," he wails. "It feels so good it can't be natural! I beg of you! I'm a *good* girl!"

"You're a slave to my pleasure, and you love it," I rasp. "You live for it. You yearn for my strong hand and throbbing cock."

The bed is shaking, and Jackson's cuffs rattle. The air stinks of masculine arousal, and it's filled with the sounds of slapping skin and desperate grunts.

"Sir, please!" Jackson yells. "I am yours. I am *yours!* Free me!"

I drop my head back and come like a champion, claiming my prize, marking my territory. "Take it, take it, *take it!*" I bellow as I spurt inside him. He clenches around me, milking every last drop from my dick. I shudder and gasp, reeling from the force of my climax. "Good girl," I whisper, rubbing up and down his back as he trembles. "Such a good girl."

Gently, I pull out. He's got to be tender after a weekend of enthusiastic and often quite rough sex, but he barely whimpers as I extract myself. I dispose of the condom and use a couple of tissues to wipe the excess lube from around my groin for comfort. Then I carefully help him to turn back around. His wrists are still bound, but now he's settled against the pillows and much more comfortable.

I move over him and touch my thumb to his chin as I kiss him deeply, tasting the sweet lip gloss. "How are you feeling, princess?"

He's shaking and sweaty. He gulps, his eyes big and desperate. "I need you, Sir," he rasps. "Please. I can't help it. I want you."

I caress the side of his neck. "I knew you would eventually," I murmur, kissing him again. "It's okay. Let me take care of you, your highness."

He whimpers as I kiss down his throat, then move down his body. I loosen the knot that's keeping the toga together, flicking it open so I can appreciate his lingerie in all its glory. I massage his tits, kissing his nipples through the material, then pushing them together against my cheeks.

My hands skim his sides as my mouth drifts down his chest and stomach, feeling his happy trail tickle against my lips. His cock is rock hard, encased in the pretty panties that I kiss it through. He moans and slowly writhes against me. I grip onto his muscular thighs.

"Be still now," I tell him. He pants as he looks down at me, but he does as he's told. "Good girl." I slip my fingers under the top of the knickers, then slide them over his hips and down his legs, casting them aside and leaving his rigid cock exposed and leaking. "So pretty."

He sobs as I lick up his shaft and wrap my lips over the head, sucking gently. "Oh, Sir," he begs. I'm going to take my time with him, though. I want to torture my prisoner a little more.

I push his legs farther apart so I can fondle his heavy balls as I suck on the end of his cock. My other hand is jerking off the base leisurely.

"So good. Don't stop," he gasps.

I can feel him trying not to move too much beneath me because he's a good boy and I told him not to. He pulls at the restraints, though, I think more to reassure us both that they're there. He's not actually disobeying me or trying to break free. He's reminding me that he's at my mercy and that until I release him, I can do what I want with him.

I alternate my pace, speeding up before slowing down, flicking my tongue and twisting my hand, using every trick I know to drive him out of his mind. He's trembling and crying when he finally begs, "Daddy, please."

My fucking heart.

I pop off and kiss the tip. "It's okay, baby boy. You can come whenever you want now."

He mewls as I swallow him deep and suck hard, determined to drag his orgasm out of him all the way from his toes. His hips buck, and he shouts out, "Daddy!"

I don't stop. I take all of his bitter cream as he starts spurting down my throat, throbbing hot and hard against my tongue. He comes and comes until I'm not sure what liquid he's even got left in his body. Finally, he sags against the bed, completely spent.

I ease off and wipe the back of my hand over my mouth. Then I crawl up the bed and swiftly uncuff his wrists, massaging them both to make sure he's not too sore. I grab a couple of tissues to mop up his intimate parts before pulling back the bed covers and dragging him against me so we can lie together, his back to my chest. I remove the cheap gold laurel so it doesn't poke me in the eye, placing it on the nightstand.

"Boy?" I say, half wondering if he's already fallen asleep. I wouldn't be surprised.

"Yes, Daddy?" he says, albeit sleepily. I know the feeling, but I need to say this before the moment passes.

"That was incredible. No one's ever done anything like that for me before. Thank you, sweet boy."

He turns his head, blinking his glittery eyes and smiling adorably up at me. "I'm so happy you liked it."

I shake my head. "No, good boy. I loved it. You were my perfect prisoner princess."

"Anytime, Daddy," he assures me, snuggling back down.

I pull the duvet back up and over us, my eyelids drooping as I succumb to a post-orgasm nap.

This young man is more incredible than I ever could have imagined.

How am I ever going to let him go?

CHAPTER 13

Jackson

THE NEXT SEVERAL WEEKS PASS IN A KIND OF BLUR. BENEDICT and I are living this wild double life where we somehow manage to keep up the illusion at work that we're just colleagues. But every weekend I'm at his place from the moment I clock off on Friday evenings until he drops me off by the dorms on Monday morning so we can arrive separately.

It's bleeding into the week as well, now. We've made out in his office many times, but it's escalated to me giving him blow jobs under his desk while I jerk off into a tissue. Just last Tuesday, he bent me over his desk and fucked me hard and fast. The door was locked but the thrill of knowing someone could knock at any time had my heart racing.

It's not just the sex, though. That's incredible, don't get me wrong. But so are lazy Sunday mornings in bed with him doing crosswords and me doing Duolingo. I love watching movies with him and making popcorn and taking Dotty out on her walks. That's still a bit risky. It worries me that someone might notice how much time we're spending together if they also frequent the woods regularly enough. But we're careful not to hold hands or kiss out in the open.

I'd be a liar if I didn't admit that wasn't getting to me slightly.

I know it was my suggestion to keep things on the down low, and I don't regret that when it comes to work. But I hate being back in the closet.

When I realized I was gay, I came out to my family right away. I don't think I was even in middle school yet. They were incredibly supportive. But I didn't want the drama and hassle from other kids, so I didn't say anything to my friends and peers (other than Selena, obviously) for a few years after that, and it was suffocating. Eventually, I had to come out, consequences be damned. Selena was there, ready and waiting to smack any fool who came at me, but in the end, it was pretty anti-climactic. People had either already guessed or didn't really care.

But I was free.

Then the same kind of shame crept in as I harbored a new secret. By the time I graduated college, I was wearing lingerie pretty much all the time unless I knew there was a chance I might be discovered. But then along came Benedict and released that burden for me as well.

Yet I can't tell anyone about him.

Well, aside from Selena.

"You did *not* dress up as a sexy alien for him?" she whispers over her peppermint mocha, her tone scandalized, but she's clearly dying for more. We're at our monthly Saturday morning Toe Beans rendezvous. I haven't gone into the psychology behind it for the sake of Benedict's privacy, but I have confessed that we like spicing things up in the bedroom with some fun role-playing.

I grin and nod, happily taking a spoon to the mountain of whipped cream and rainbow sprinkles sitting on top of my hot chocolate. "He was the sexy scientist who discovered me."

I leave out the part where he was going to impregnate me to save both our species, whether I liked it or not. I'm not entirely sure why the idea of being a broodmare is so fucking hot to me, but it is. I guess it's another layer in the non-con fantasies we both yearn for.

I know it's probably conceited, but I'm so proud of myself for coming up with that little plan. We still play at being student and teacher. It's our go-to. (The schoolgirl's grades are really bad. She's having to suck a lot of cock to maintain her GPA, haha.) But the more colorful storylines seem to have done the trick in freeing Benedict from the guilt-ridden prison he'd made for himself.

What he desires isn't wrong. Certainly not with the way he makes me feel.

The alien scene was the first one he properly collared me, too. It's just a simple length of soft black leather with silver rings and fastenings, but the way it made me shiver and salivate when he slipped it around my neck and chained me to his bed...*urgh.*

He'll often use one of his ties if he starts the scene in a suit, and I still like that as well. But he bought the collar specifically for me, and that makes my tummy feel all funny and wonderful. Either way, when he puts something around my neck, I feel owned and claimed in all the best ways.

I waggle my eyebrows at my bestie. "There was another time I was a mermaid, and he was a pirate captain who'd captured me in his net."

I try not to squirm in my seat. We got a hell of a lot of mileage out of that scenario, because all the pirates wanted a turn fucking the mermaid, and she was fascinated and obsessed with humans, happy to study all of them *very* intimately.

Selena does squirm, a delighted look on her face. "So I was right. He gets the *lingerie.*"

She whispers the last word, even though the chances of anyone hearing us over the cacophony of conversations is unlikely. The only one who might is Lizzie, the stunning but shy fluffy gray cat, who's watching me again with her enormous blue eyes. I think my secrets are safe with her, though.

It's bad. Obviously, I want her to find a forever home. But I'm also really happy she's still here, and she's crept over to be near us again. There's just something about her I'm drawn to.

"Yes, you were right," I say, rolling my eyes. We talked about this at our last coffee date, too. But I didn't confess to all the role-playing and the fact that I actually really enjoy being a girl sometimes.

It's certainly thrown up some interesting questions for me. When I was the mermaid, I bought myself a shiny, iridescent bluey-green skirt that hangs halfway down my thighs and fans out when I spin around. I just sort of…started wearing it around Benedict's apartment. He didn't comment on it other than to say I was his pretty boy, which gave me the good kind of butterflies.

I like the way it makes me feel, though. The same when I paint my nails and wear a little makeup. I haven't really dared do any of that stuff outside of Benedict's home—not yet. He's my safe space. But I wonder if sometime soon I might brave the outside world with some more feminine attire.

"He definitely gets it a lot," I say to Selena, smirking at my own innuendo.

Now she rolls her eyes. "So let me get this right. He's amazing in bed, loves your kink, a perfect Daddy, and handsome AF. Did I miss anything?"

I sigh and push some crumbs around my plate. "Only the part where he's leaving next month."

She clicks her tongue. "That was actually going to be my point. Have you guys talked about it?"

"What's there to talk about?" I ask with a shrug. "He's going home. We agreed right from the start that this would just be a short-term thing."

Her stare is withering. "Yeah, but that was before you went and fell in L-O-V-E."

I throw a napkin at her, but it just makes her laugh. "I'm not in love," I grumble.

"You are in Egypt, though, because you're *in denial*," she quips.

I can't help but laugh at her terrible pun. "You'll make an excellent dad one day," I inform her.

She reaches out and squeezes my hand. "Seriously, babe. I can see you're crazy about him. You guys spend every possible damn minute together. You might not want to use the L word, but the feelings are clearly strong. Isn't that worth at least having a conversation about?"

I shrug and look up at my kitty friend. "I'm not sure it is," I say glumly.

I hate to admit it, but she might be just a little bit right.

I promised myself that I wouldn't catch feelings. There was always a time limit on this fling. But I'm besotted with him. Even when we're not together, we talk and text all the time. I know he was worried about trying out being a Daddy, but he takes care of me exactly the way I dreamed. He looks after me when we're at home, and even goes so far as deciding things like what lingerie I should wear or what I should pack for lunch. Even better is when he *makes* me lunch.

Not to mention when he fucks me in the underwear he's selected especially for me.

Yeah…maybe the L word is creeping in. But why have that conversation? Him going home isn't negotiable. I'd rather keep my feelings a little hidden and avoid the total heartbreak that will come from him telling me that I'm not worth staying in Paddle Creek for.

And that's *okay*, I remind myself. Oxford is his home. He only came out here to care for his mom, which was so amazing and lovely of him to do, and now that chapter in his life is coming to an end. I can't expect him to change his whole life plan for me. That would be insane. We've only been seeing each other for a couple of months. That's no length of time to alter the whole course of his life.

It's fine.

Yeah, I'll probably be crying into tubs of ice cream for a while, but he's already shown me that it's possible to have the kind of relationship I want and not have to hide the sexiest, kinkiest parts of me.

The chances of finding anybody as perfect as Benedict are probably pretty slim, especially here in Paddle Creek. But that's a problem for future me. The point is it *is* possible. I'm not a dirty freak who's going to die alone. There's nothing wrong with a man like me wanting to feel pretty and feminine, and I'm not going to stop.

Even when Benedict leaves.

Selena pats my hand then releases it to sip her coffee. "Just…promise me you'll keep it in mind, hmm? I know you probably want to avoid a difficult conversation because you're a baby, but you don't actually *know* what's going on in his head."

"I'm not a baby," I pout.

She grins. "How's your rainbow sparkle hot choccie?"

"Fucking delicious," I say proudly, taking a sip of my super sweet drink.

Okay, so maybe she has a point. I'm trying to protect

myself from any more pain on top of what I know is coming my way already. But I am just assuming Benedict's feelings and plans are still the same. Perhaps I could dance around the issue and test the waters? That wouldn't be the worst plan. Even if it's to confirm that he's definitely still planning on heading home. At least then I'd know for sure.

I open my mouth to continue giving my best friend a hard time, but I'm interrupted by the sudden appearance of a fluffy gray cloud right in front of my face.

Oh my god.

Lizzie has jumped from her perch to come join us. Selena gasps and wastes no time in whipping out her phone, presumably to take photos. I, on the other hand, hold my breath and very carefully raise my hand to let her sniff my fingers to gain more trust. Then I try gently stroking her back.

"She's purring," I whisper, absolutely delighted. "Oh, my heart. Hi, baby. Are you the sweetest girl?" She looks up at me with her huge blue eyes, then picks her way around my plate and mug before hopping onto my lap.

I really do stop breathing, terrified of scaring her off.

"Wow," Selena says. Then she lowers her phone and turns it to show me. She wasn't taking photos. She was filming. I watch the video back, moved by the emotion on my own face and in my voice.

"Thank you for capturing that," I say softly, daring to pet Lizzie again. She's motoring away on my thighs, apparently quite content.

"No worries," she says smugly. "I've already sent it to you. Promise me you'll forward it to your Daddy, so he's reminded of how madly in love he is with you."

I roll my eyes, wishing that were true. But I probably will send it to him anyway because it's made me ridiculously happy, and I want to share that with him. I want to share everything with him.

I look down at my beautiful cat friend, aware that our hour-long reservation is almost up. Someone else will need the table, and we'll have to go. But I don't want to have to move her or leave her behind.

But I guess that's life, isn't it? People move on. Others get left behind.

I pretend I'm only sad about me and the cat, and not me and my Daddy. It doesn't work, but I give myself top marks for effort.

In the end, I'm going to have to say good-bye to both Lizzie and Benedict.

And fuck if it isn't going to hurt like hell.

CHAPTER 14
Benedict

I can't stop watching the bloody cat video.

It's the utter delight on Jackson's face when that gray fur baby appears in front of him. Having always had dogs, it's taking me a while to wrap my head around cat psychology. But I can't deny there's something incredible that comes from this timid creature saying, 'I choose *you*.' It's a gift. An honor.

Kind of like when a brilliant young man chooses you to share his deepest, darkest desires with.

It's a Saturday, so he's here at my place as usual. We have broken the routine to see other friends or if errands need doing, but for the most part, he simply moves in every Friday night then leaves again each Monday morning.

Yet it still doesn't feel like enough.

I hate having to ignore him at work. Or at least, keep my distance when we're not behind closed doors. Logically, I can still see it's for the best. I'm sure Bobbi is on to us in some form or another. The less she knows about me defiling her godson, the better. I just want to hold his hand and fix his hair and put my hand on his lower back without having to think about who's around or what might happen if they found out.

Something I've come to appreciate is that secrets aren't all that sexy. Being *free* of them is.

But I've only got a matter of weeks left here in town—a couple of months at most. I couldn't possibly blow up Jackson's life, then leave him to deal with the fallout. That would be unconscionable.

No. It's best if we carry on as usual. Part of that is also me vehemently ignoring the fact that I *am* going to be getting on a plane soon with a one-way ticket. In the moments when I have been more inclined to accept reality, I've found myself daydreaming that I might come and visit. I have another reason besides Jackson, which would make the expense of such a trip more acceptable.

Maybe.

Whatever. That other reason has been on my mind all morning, and I've decided it might be crossing a line, but I don't want to leave town without doing something about it. I hope Jackson understands.

"Do you want to take a drive with me?" I ask. He's been watching TV on the sofa after we had lunch, and he looks up with happiness in his eyes.

"Sure!" he cries. Then he looks down at his outfit.

I've done my best to be supportive without trying to make too big a deal of it, but it's not escaped my notice how monumental it is that he's been wearing skirts around my place. It started with that blue metallic one, but then he got himself a couple of warmer pleated ones in black and cream. They hang just above his knee, and he looks so stylish. I'm a firm believer that people should wear whatever the hell they like, but I have to say seeing him in a skirt doesn't even look unusual. He carries it effortlessly.

But that's all been here, at home, with me so far.

"I should change," he says softly.

I shrug, wanting to encourage him but not push him. "It's still a little nippy out. You could put some leggings on underneath to keep you warm, perhaps? There won't be many people where we're going."

I watch him as he frowns and nibbles his lip. "Yeah…" he says slowly. "And I'd be wearing a coat. Would that be okay with you?"

My heart aches, and I go over to pull him off the sofa and into my arms. "Of course it is, baby boy," I say with deep fondness. I want to say that I'm proud to be seen with him no matter what he's wearing, but our continuing need for secrecy somewhat spoils that sentiment, so I leave it unsaid.

He gives me a sweet smile and a kiss, then heads to the bedroom to amend his outfit.

I tell Dotty she has to stay here but that we'll be back soon. Her face drops, but I'm sure she'll wait by the door the whole time we're gone and be ecstatic to see us upon our return, and then she'll forget she was ever left behind.

We're quiet on the drive. I think Jackson senses my mood, and I love that he's respectful of me needing a little calmness right now. When we stop off at the florists in town and I buy a pretty pink mixed bouquet, I think he probably guesses where we're headed.

"Is this okay?" I ask as I pull the car up in the cemetery's parking lot.

He reaches over and squeezes my hand. "Of *course* it is," he says, and I realize we've mirrored our conversation just now about his skirt. I feel such a strong pang of affection for him I get a little tight in my throat. But I cough and shake it off. I know him by now. It shouldn't be a surprise that he's kind and thoughtful and supportive.

He really is wonderful.

We each exit the car, and I lead the way to where my mother's grave lies. I've kept it as nicely maintained as I can, and it hurts me to think I'll be leaving her behind when I return to Oxford. But for now, I bend down and sweep off some dried leaves and replace the old flowers with the new.

I rest my hand on the top of her headstone and take a moment to remember her smile and her warm hands. The way she'd always get the punchline wrong on a joke because she was already too busy laughing at herself to tell it right. How excited she'd get about Christmas, especially if it snowed.

I wrestle between wishing we'd spent more time together as adults and feeling gratitude that I upended my life to be with her when it mattered the most.

"Tell me about her," Jackson says quietly as I straighten up again. We've both got our hands in our pockets—even now afraid that someone might see if we were to get too close—but he bumps his shoulder against mine affectionately.

I sigh. "She had a lot of friends," I say, which was true. I'm more like my dad in that I'm content with just a few close friends or my own company, but Mum loved people. "She ran a book club that definitely involved as much drinking wine as it did reading books. She did art classes and was in a choir." I shake my head, fresh grief washing over me like little waves against the shore. "She had an amazing voice and would always fight to get the best solos."

Jackson laughs, and so do I, reminding myself that it's okay to be happy as well as sad.

"She led a full life. I wish she'd had a bit more time—especially with my dad. That was a terrible shock to her. I can understand now why she came back home to Paddle Creek. She needed both a new start as well as somewhere familiar."

"It's why I came back," Jackson agrees softly.

I'm glad his return home wasn't shrouded in grief, though. A sudden urge to protect him from the whole world rushes through me, and god damn it, I don't care if anyone's around. I pull him into a hug that he readily accepts, squeezing me tightly. People need comforting at gravesides. If anyone sees anything, that's what I can say was happening. For now, I just enjoy having my lover openly in my arms for once.

"I miss her," I confess as we naturally ease apart and look down at her name carved into the stone. "Sometimes I catch myself reaching for the phone to call her. I still have her number saved. Isn't that silly?"

Jackson frowns and shakes his head. "I don't think that's silly at all," he says. "Whatever brings you comfort. Grief is so tricky. You shouldn't do anything until you're ready. You don't have to move on by anyone else's schedule, only your own."

I manage a smile for him. "Thank you," I say genuinely. I don't think he's suffered a big loss of his own—certainly not one he's mentioned to me. I think he's just got a lot of empathy, which in my opinion is an admirable quality in a person.

We stand there a little longer. I tell him about some of the holidays we took when I was a child, and reminisce about her incredible lasagna recipe, which I'm very thankful she handed down the secrets of before she left.

I sigh and look around the cemetery. Spring is creeping closer, and it's a bright if blustery day. I see one of the groundskeepers puttering around in the distance, grateful that her grave won't be allowed to grow wild at least.

I wonder if Jackson follows my line of sight and guesses my train of thought from what he says next. "If you like, I could pop over here and see her sometimes. You know— when you're gone."

I swallow. Both of us seem to be stubbornly refusing to

discuss my departure and rarely bring it up. But this is important, and in this moment, I'm very thankful he had the courage to do so.

"That would be lovely," I say thickly, nodding and looking at her flowers. If I look at him, the tears burning at the back of my eyes might spill, and I'd hate to put that burden on him. I'm the Daddy Dom. I'm supposed to look after him, not the other way around. But he appears to have not gotten that memo because he slips his arm around me and places a brazen kiss on my cheek. That's against the rules, but right now, I don't give a shit.

"Of course, Daddy," he whispers.

I ache with every fiber of my being. For a fleeting second, I imagine that I could stay. I wouldn't have to leave my mother, but more importantly, I wouldn't have to leave Jackson either.

But I'm being ridiculous. The plan was always to go home to Oxford. That's where my *life* is. I have my job and my friends just waiting for me to pick up where I left off two and a half years ago.

Jackson is so young. He's got his whole life ahead of him. He won't want me to change all my plans and put the pressure on him for something long-term. This works so well precisely because there isn't any pressure. We're living in a dream bubble that isn't sustainable. If I stayed, we wouldn't be able to keep living this secret double life. It would fall apart.

No, I need to stay strong. Yes, my feelings for him are growing stronger by the day. But once I'm back home, I'm sure the infatuation will fade. He deserves someone who he can be out and proud with. He deserves to date a lot of guys to find one he really loves, not be burdened by staying with the first guy he opened up to about his more feminine side.

I have to set him free.

And as much as it kills me, that probably means booking my plane ticket sooner rather than later.

CHAPTER 15

Jackson

AT THE MOMENT, I'M RESOLUTELY PUSHING DOWN MY feelings about Benedict finally booking his plane ticket by giving myself something else to worry about. I'm standing in front of my mirror in a pair of combat boots, a black skirt, a white shirt with the sleeves rolled up, and a simple leather necklace with a silver clasp that's sitting in the dip of my throat. It's not quite my collar, but the pressure on my throat makes me feel like I'm with my Daddy anyway.

I think it's kind of subtle as far as looks go. I could be wearing a kilt at a glance, and people are generally okay with those. But if I'm being honest, this is monumental.

I'm going to wear a skirt out in public.

I know I did last weekend with Benedict, but that was to a quiet location, and I had a long coat over the top. Tonight, I'm going to the Ice Cream Parlor with Selena, and there will definitely be a lot of people there.

I'm trying to tell myself that a gay bar should be the perfect place to try this out. It should be safe. But it's gay guys who have made me feel like shit about this in the past.

Who have scared me with violent threats. I'm not sure I can guarantee I'll be okay.

But what in life *is* a guarantee? Nothing is certain, and I'm tired of hiding.

I'll be with Selena, but I also want a bit more reassurance to carry with me as I take this slightly terrifying step. So I spend ages taking photos of my reflection until there's one I'm happy with. Then I open up my messages.

JACKSON: What do you think, Daddy?

I chew my lip nervously as I look at the picture I've just sent, feeling vulnerable as I wait for his approval. I know I should have more confidence in myself and my decisions, but I can't help it. I'm not Selena. If Daddy says I look okay, then that will give me the boost I need to step out of my dorm room.

I almost fall off the bed as the reply comes through, and I hastily jab my fingers at the phone to open it up.

BENEDICT: You look STUNNING, baby boy. Have an amazing time tonight. I can't wait to hear all about it.

My heart sings.

"Okay, then," I say out loud to myself as I send back a heart emoji. "You can do this. You're going to be okay."

I spend another five minutes adding final touches to my look. Another spritz of aftershave. Another poke at my hair. One last check that my subtle eyeliner hasn't smudged.

Before I can chicken out, I grab my wallet and keys, putting them in a small black backpack that I sling over my shoulders, then force myself out the door.

I'm wearing my coat again, partly because it's cold and partly because it hides my outfit for now. It's one thing to be brave in a queer space. It's another to just walk out into town, not knowing who might take offense at my attire and decide I need a punch.

But as I step onto the streetcar—no drinking and driving

for me, baby—the driver glances over just as the wind catches my coat, opening it up to show off my legs.

She whistles. "Damn, pumpkin. You gonna break some hearts tonight."

I blush, a little embarrassed, sure, but mostly with pride. "Thanks," I say before paying my fair, then hurrying down the trolley to find a seat. Okay. Someone saw my skirt and thought I looked cool. That's a pretty good start to the night, right?

I text Selena to let her know I'm on my way, hoping she's already there. I don't want to keep her waiting long if I don't have to, but also, she's badass. No one's going to bother her. I on the other hand, would really rather not be the one hanging out by myself right now.

I take a long, deep breath in and then slowly let it out. I'll be fine. I just need to keep my wits about me. I'm not putting my earbuds in now, and I'm not going to drink too much so I'm aware of my surroundings on the journey home. And if anyone does try something, I am still quite big and scary if I put my mind to it, even with my fabulous legs out.

I just…I don't want anyone's bullshit. I don't want anyone to get angry or threatened because I'm wearing something that surprises them. It's not erotic. Hell, I've seen girls in skirts so short I can see what they had for lunch. At Halloween, it's perfectly acceptable to go out in little more than your underwear—if you're female *or* male—and that's fine. My outfit by comparison is pretty tame.

I drum my fingers on my knee. I can't control if people are small-minded. I can only control my happiness, and since that's on a cliff edge right now, thanks to the Benedict situation, I need to protect it at all costs.

He was always going to leave. That's what makes this relationship work, I'm sure. We've both been brave because we know if it all falls apart, it was only going to last a couple of months anyway.

Except it's not falling apart. It's going from strength to strength. And I know without a doubt that when he gets on that plane, my heart is going to break clean in two.

That's why it's so important I take everything I can from the special connection we have and make it strong so the parts I can keep will survive once he's gone. I'm not going to accept another man into my bed who doesn't see all of my intimate desires and is okay with them. No—not okay— fucking loves them. And if I can finally get brave and start showing my femininity on the outside, that might just do everyone a favor and announce my kinks in advance, not to mention make me feel content in my own skin.

Because when I push away all the fear and anxiety, I know I look killer in this outfit.

I thank the driver with her enormous afro as I go to step off the trolley. "Go get 'em, tiger!" she calls out after me, making me grin. I guess getting off at this stop makes it pretty obvious that I'm going to Creams, ie the kind of place a guy might wear a skirt to.

I snort to myself as I think of Toole's, the only other gay bar around these parts. Actually, it's not a bar but an Irish pub frequented by older guys, usually bear types. It's definitely more of a sit-down-and-drink-beer vibe, which sometimes I'm into. But tonight, I want to twirl in my skirt, drink fruity cocktails, and let off steam.

I greet the fabulous doorman, Dijon. He's not the bouncer. As far as I can tell, his job is mainly to look stunning in four-inch heels, sparkle, say hello to everyone, then check if there's anything you need. The guy has already got to be six foot before the platform boots, and has the shoulders of a linebacker. He definitely doesn't seem to care what anyone thinks of him in a negative way. Otherwise, he wouldn't go to all that effort every night. I feel bold enough to unbutton my coat as I walk up the street and approach the door, and I'm rewarded as he gives me a look up and down before whistling.

"Well, hello there, handsome," he purrs, snapping his fingers with long red press-on nails. "You have a good night."

I grin as I nod at the bouncer and let him take a peek inside my mostly empty bag. "Thanks," I say to both him and Dijon, feeling braver by the minute.

It's not too busy, so I see Selena waiting at the bar almost right away. I'd run the idea of my outfit by her, but her face still lights up when she sees me. "Wow, babe," she cries as I make my way over to her, and we kiss cheeks. "I am loving this so much for you."

I grin, confident enough to slip my coat off and drape it off the stool, fishing my wallet out of my mini backpack to order a drink. I might be buzzing from three people complimenting me in a row, but some liquid courage won't hurt either.

"Can I get a porn star martini?" I ask the bartender, who nods and sets about mixing it.

I settle on the stool and exhale loudly before looking over at Selena. "So how are you?"

She waves her finger at me and arches a perfectly sculpted eyebrow. "Nuh-uh. You didn't drag me out here on the damn Tuesday open mic night to ask how I am. Some chick was just reading poetry, and it was *bad.* She was hot… but that's not the point. You have to tell me what's going on with you before that dude with the guitar gets up. He's not even hot." She squints. "Well…maybe…"

I snort and roll my eyes. Selena is the least picky person I know when it comes to the looks and personalities of hookups, especially with men. It's how she finds the truly awful ones, so I sigh and decide I better bear all and save her from being too captivated by Mr. Guitar.

"I just felt like the time was right to step outside my comfort zone and be more my authentic self," I say before thanking the bartender as he places my drink down. I pay for it, then glance = back to find Selena looking at me with raised eyebrows.

"And this change of attitude is thanks to your amazing, loving Daddy?"

I try not to squirm guiltily in my seat. "Yeah," I agree lightly.

"Because you're wildly in love."

I do my best not to flinch at the L word, but she definitely notices and gives me an even harder stare.

"Because he's booked his ticket back to the UK, and I'm feeling totally normal and okay about that," I mumble into my martini glass.

She throws her hands up. "You haven't told him how you feel, have you?" she cries in frustration. But then she narrows her eyes. "Or you did, and he booked the flight anyway."

"No!" I say quickly, but then realize the first option isn't much better. However, at least Benedict isn't fleeing from me because he got so freaked out by my feelings.

But he is still leaving.

"I told you," I say with a sigh, sipping my drink and appreciating the first hit of alcohol. "This was always the plan. It's just a fling. He has to go home. If he doesn't keep working at the college, then he can't keep his visa."

She frowns. "The college wouldn't be mad if he stayed, though, right? Hasn't he revolutionized the classics department?"

Someone behind me scoffs. "Roberta Schultz would tie Benedict Knight to a chair if it would make him stay. She's even found him a pay rise that she found the money for from somewhere, but he's being a stubborn ass."

My eyes go wide as I twist on the barstool to see a young woman, I guess in her early thirties in a long black skirt, a shiny black corset cinching her waist, and a black ruffled top completing the slightly morbid look. Her curly hair is piled on top of her head, and she looks at me through sparkly horn-rimmed glasses as she raises a glass of red wine to her dark lips.

"Oh," I say as recognition hits. I don't spend much time in the library, but I've heard several tall tales about the librarian who's supposedly also a witch. I'm not afraid of a goth, but I am slightly perturbed that a member of staff might have overheard our conversation.

Scratch that. I've immediately broken out into a sweat, and my heart is thumping in my chest.

"Ms. Maude," I practically squeak. "Uh, I—"

She arches an eyebrow. "Relax. You're not going to have a heart attack today." Her gaze flicks around me like she's looking for something. "No, definitely not."

"About what my friend and I said about Professor Knight. Uh. I'm his TA, and—"

"You've been having fantastic sex since the new year," she says, rolling her eyes and tapping her fingernail against her glass. "Your auras couldn't speak any louder. Don't worry. I suspect most people won't notice."

I open and close my mouth. "Oh. Okay," I say, unsure where to take this conversation now. So…she knows but doesn't seem particularly concerned. And more importantly, reckons other people won't know. We've been so *careful* at work. What does she mean by 'auras,' anyway?

She leans to the side of me and quirks the corner of her mouth at Selena. "Let me guess. He's head over heels but hasn't actually *told* Knight this?"

Selena throws her hands up. "No, he has not! He seems convinced there's nothing he can do and that he just has to suffer in silence instead of talking like a grownup."

"There *isn't* any point," I mutter, not really enjoying being ganged up on.

"Men," Ms. Maude says, sipping from her glass again, her gaze lingering on Selena before sliding over to the small stage. Her whole face lights up. I realize the guy with the guitar is settling on a stool in front of the mic. "Speaking of which. Oh. This is going to be *painful.*"

She drifts away, a serene look on her spooky face, leaving me with my best friend, whose mouth is hanging open.

"I...I think I might be in love," she croaks, her gaze following Paddle Creek's mysterious librarian.

I sigh as the guy starts playing basic chords on the guitar, his lyrics so cringe about angels and butterflies and possibly puppies that I wince and immediately block them out.

In love, yeah.

I think I might know a thing or two about that.

No. No! I can't think like that. It's just going to hurt me more. If Benedict has been offered a pay rise and still said no, that means he's truly set on going home to England. Paddle Creek isn't where he belongs. He's too big for somewhere like here, and he's already given it three years. A mind as great as his deserves to go back to one of the most prestigious universities in the world.

How can I compete with that?

What we've had has been life-changing. I'll never forget it. But it's time to admit that it's coming to its natural conclusion, and that's okay. Benedict has taught me a huge amount. I know I'm going to demand so much for myself moving forward.

I'll miss him like crazy, but I'll carry a part of him with me always if I honor him by living my authentic life. He'll be there every time I wear a skirt or put on makeup. Every single set of lingerie will have different memories associated with them of how he fucked me in them. How he worshiped me in them.

It's going to suck, but I'll be okay.

So long as I don't say I'm in love out loud, then it won't be real and can't hurt me as much.

Right?

CHAPTER 16

Benedict

I KNOW THE MOOD HAS SHIFTED AS SOON AS I OPEN MY FRONT door. The fact that Jackson's rung the bell instead of letting himself in says a lot. Actually, the fact that I'm home before him and haven't found him draped on my bed in some sort of fabulous outfit says even more.

That fucking plane ticket is hanging over our heads like the sword of Damocles.

"Hey, baby boy," I say softly.

"Hey, Daddy," he replies in the same tone.

He steps inside, and I close the door, then wrap my arms around him. I know this has to hurt. He's got to be feeling rejected. I want to tell him that it's not his fault. This is just what I have to do. I have to go home, and that means setting him free. I know he's just infatuated because this is his first proper exploration of kink.

But that doesn't mean I don't care deeply for him.

I've wondered several times if I could ask him to come visit or if he'd be interested in me visiting him. But I don't want to confuse things, not right now. I feel bad enough as it is. Maybe once I'm settled back at home, we can discuss options about keeping in touch, but then again, if I want him to move on, it will probably be better if I let him go and give him the chance to find someone new.

'Want' is doing a lot of heavy lifting in that line of thought. I don't *want* him to move on or find someone new. But I think that's what's in his best interests, and as his Daddy, that's my main concern.

In the future, it will be at least. All I want to do now is make him feel cherished.

"Come here," I murmur.

I rub his back before releasing him, then reach to take his hand. He drops his weekend bag by the door, where Dotty goes to sniff it immediately like she hasn't inspected it a hundred times before. She wags her tail, then trots off to the living room. Even she's quiet.

I lead Jackson to the bedroom and close the door. I grip his shoulders, and he places his hands on my hips, almost like we're going to dance. We do sway on the spot for a moment, our temples pressed together. I inhale deeply, wishing I could bottle up his scent. These last few weeks are going to be tough.

But this isn't a funeral. No one has been lost, not really. Once we get through the worst of it, we'll remember this time with such fond tenderness, I'm sure.

"Don't be sad, baby boy," I say as I nuzzle our cheeks against one another. "It's going to be okay."

He gives a shaky laugh and nods against me. "I know. I'm just in my feelings. I'll get over it."

"Would you allow me to help you?" I ask.

He nods again, so I kiss a trail along his jaw until I find his mouth. Our lips meet gently over and over again, savoring the moment. There are no games tonight, just two people who want to be close to one another. Who want to hold each other and kiss away the other's tears.

I start steering him toward the bed, not in any rush. We have all evening, all night, all weekend. As our legs bump against the mattress, I pause to pull his hoodie off, and his T-shirt comes with it, revealing a pretty white bralette.

"Would you like to keep this on?" I ask, caressing it and his skin around it.

He shakes his head. "Not tonight," he says. "I don't want anything between us."

I swallow and nod in agreement.

I always thought that I kept clothes on for a sense of power with my subs. It's different in the shower than in bed. Jackson's seen me completely starkers dozens of times. But we've never made love like that.

In this moment, I think maybe it wasn't just about me having more power. I think it was me protecting myself. Keeping a barrier to separate me from my desires. Even now, after all this time with Jackson.

I don't want anything between us tonight, either.

I slip his bra straps over his shoulders then reach around to fiddle with the clasp. I must admit that I've had very little practice with this particular maneuver. Jackson's been the first person I've gotten naked with who's worn one, but he always keeps it on. And when he undresses to get in the shower or whatever, he deals with it in a second. But I want to do this now. I need to.

Mercifully, the lingerie gods are on my side, and I manage to release the hooks and eyes without too much trouble. I'd have hated if it had broken the mood. He seems oddly vulnerable now, standing before me without the familiar satin and lace framing his chest.

I carefully take his hands and guide them to my shirt. I took my tie off before he arrived. Otherwise, that would be the only thing I'd be tempted to leave him wearing. I love putting it around his neck when we're playing, even more so than the collar we bought.

For now, I encourage Jackson to undo my buttons as I work on freeing my belt. I drop it to the floor, then unhurriedly pop the button on his jeans, then lower the zipper, revealing his pretty panties. No garters today. My boy wanted to look good, but he's not putting on a show. I get that.

When he's dropped my shirt to the floor, I ease down his knickers and jeans, pulling off his socks as I crouch to the floor. Then I run my hands back up his legs and hips as I stand, feeling the warmth of his skin.

"Lie on the bed, pretty boy," I tell him with a sweet kiss on his lips. He crawls onto the mattress and lies down on his back with his head on the pillows, watching me as I swiftly remove my own trousers and underwear.

And just like that, there's nothing left between us. I want it to stay that way.

We've been using condoms this whole time. We haven't even mentioned getting tested or going bareback, probably because that would flirt too dangerously with the idea that this could be long term. Keeping the protection reminded us —me at least—that this always had an end date. Even though I've not been with anyone else and I'm pretty sure Jackson hasn't either, I don't want to risk anything tonight. There are still ways we can be skin-to-skin intimate, though.

I lie down on my side of the bed, then pull Jackson against me, his back to my chest and his head resting on my bicep. I feel like I'm protecting him like this as I wrap my arms around his front and lean down for a kiss that he so willingly gives me.

I'm his Daddy, and I'm going to take care of him.

For a while we just lie together, snuggling and feeling the heat radiating off our bodies. His kisses are so sweet, like him, but eventually a hunger starts to grow between us, the fire building from an ember to a fierce glow.

I trail my hand down his hard abs and tease him just a little by caressing his thighs. I still want my boy desperate for me. He whimpers, and the noise pierces my heart. I love all those precious sounds he gives me so freely.

I don't play with him for long. His cock is already half-hard and leaking from the tip. I swipe my palm over it, capturing the pearl of liquid to help me glide over his shaft. He moans and bucks into my hand.

"Shh," I soothe him. "Daddy's going to take care of you. Just lie still."

He nods and looks up at me with those big, beautiful eyes, his lashes a little spiky with unshed tears. I only want him to cry from pleasure tonight.

I kiss his mouth and jaw and neck as I leisurely stroke him off. He's grinding his butt against me, giving me some friction, but I need more. Now that he's hard and needy for me, I can take more. But like I said, I want nothing at all between us tonight.

"Move a little for Daddy, good boy," I say as I briefly let him go. I use my hand to encourage his legs apart a few inches, then arrange myself so my hard dick slides between his thighs. I close him back up again and retake his cock in my hand, then slowly start to thrust between his legs against his taint and balls, my precum helping the glide.

"Oh, oh," he utters as we undulate together, moving like one creature, a slippery writhing mass of pleasure.

"Good boy," I say as I kiss and suck and bite on his neck. "So good for Daddy. So perfect."

"Daddy," he moans as I pick up the pace with my hand. I'm not chasing my orgasm. For once, he's going to come first, and I'm going to love watching every second of it. My cock feels amazing wrapped up tight between his legs, and it can happily throb there until I grant it its release.

"Good boy," I say over and over again. He's thrashing back against me now, gasping and screwing up his face.

"Yes, yes, *yes!* Don't stop, Daddy. Don't stop!"

I have no intention of it. I jerk him off faster, sucking on his earlobe until I rasp in his ear. "Come for me, beautiful boy. Come for Daddy."

He grits his teeth for a few seconds, then arches his back, cum spitting all over the duvet and my hand. He wails and shakes against me as I wring him dry, milking every last drop from his gorgeous cock.

Slowly, he starts to come down, his body limp against mine. I kiss his cheek. "Stay right there, baby," I whisper.

I ease my length out from between his legs and take myself in hand, the tip of my cock bumping against where his thigh meets the perfect curve of his plump arse. It only takes a few strokes before I'm shooting my load, thick ropes of cream painting his bum and the backs of his legs.

I take in a few lungfuls as I come back down, then I hug him tightly to me, mess be damned. He wriggles around in my grasp until we're facing each other, and then he's kissing me with such earnest emotion it takes my breath away. "Thank you, Daddy," he says, clinging to my neck like a life raft, our legs tangled together. "Thank you."

"You're so welcome, baby boy," I tell him back.

It doesn't seem enough, but those are the words that will have to do for now.

God damn it. I'm going to miss being his Daddy so much it might just kill me.

CHAPTER 17

Jackson

THE NEXT FEW WEEKS ARE SLIGHTLY BETTER. OUR TENDER lovemaking session gave me a kind of preemptive closure on the whole situation and has enabled me to stop moping around. Mostly. There will be life after Benedict Knight, even though right now, it seems kind of impossible to imagine.

But at least I'm not wasting what time I have left with him. I've been lucky to have had this chance. It might never have happened at all if we hadn't taken that crazy scary leap toward each other.

Besides, spring is in full force here in Paddle Creek, and it's hard to keep up such misery when the days are getting longer and brighter. It's one of the reasons I've decided to walk to Benedict's place this evening rather than taking the streetcar. I never drive on the slim chance someone might recognize my car.

Speaking of which, I've been paying even more attention to other members of the faculty around campus. Benedict and I have been extra careful not to show any PDA, even when we think we're alone. Closed doors only. There don't seem to be any sideways glances or whispers going on. Still, I did pop by the library to see if I could maybe have a chat with Ms. Maude to ease my mind.

She stared at me for a full twenty seconds before handing me a pink crystal and telling me to let Sagittarius guide my way. I said I wasn't sure what that meant, but she just walked into her office with her black cat by her feet. That first-year kid, Gabe Visoth, happened to be studying at a nearby desk with his two football player boyfriends. "It means stop being a dumbass," the big one, Marty, cried out with a cheerful wave.

I can't say the interaction reassured me completely that she hasn't told anyone, but I have kept the crystal on my bedside table ever since, just in case.

I know she thinks the same as Selena in that I should pour my heart out to Benedict, but it feels *so* disrespectful to him and what we've shared these past few months. He's made his decision, and he's going home. Me groveling at his feet won't change anything.

What would I even ask him? To stay? That's crazy now he's booked his ticket, not to mention selfish. But…okay. I'm thinking that we haven't said we'll stop talking when he gets back to England, so I'm going to casually keep on messaging to start with. Then, I'm realllllly hoping he'll invite me out to visit or something.

That's as much as I'm allowing myself to hope now. I know the reality is that out of sight, out of mind is definitely a real phenomenon. But I can't bring myself to fully believe that once he gets on that plane, it'll be completely over.

I shake myself and turn my head toward the sunshine. "Happy thoughts, happy thoughts," I mumble under my breath. I have a life outside of Benedict. I'm more than who I date.

But I'd be a fool not to realize this is probably going to be one of the saddest things to ever happen to me.

"Those aren't happy thoughts, are they?" I tell myself through a forced smile.

I have to laugh. If my past self had anticipated how complicated this was all going to get, I'm not sure he would have jerked off *quite* as much to his hot new boss.

I can't say I regret a single minute of any of it, though.

I let myself into the building, then use my key to get into the apartment. "Hello?" I call out. Benedict asked me to come over a little later than usual but didn't say why. I hope everything's okay or that he's even here at all.

"In here," he calls out, answering that particular question.

I pull off my shoes, drop my bag on the floor, then hang up my coat. The bedroom door is closed, but it sounded like Benedict's voice came from the living room. In fact, I swear I can hear Dotty's snuffling and whimpers from the bedroom. What's going on? Has Benedict got something kinky in mind?

I don't think so. He'd have used his Dom voice and called me a good boy or a naughty girl or something. Still, my curiosity is piqued as I pad down the hallway and into the living room.

I find Benedict sitting on the floor, which makes me raise my eyebrows. That's not like him at all. Then I notice he's holding some kind of ribbon on a stick, confusing me even more. But he just grins at me, flicking his eyebrows before moving his gaze toward the window. Or the window*sill*, I should say.

And what's sitting on it.

I gasp as my hands fly over my mouth. It's the fluffy gray cat from Toe Beans, Lizzie. She's hunkered down in a loaf shape, looking suspiciously around the room. When she sees me, her eyes fixate, but her tail starts swishing back and forth.

"What's going on?" I whisper to Benedict, even though I can't tear myself from looking away from the kitty.

He gets to his feet and wraps an arm around me, kissing my temple. "I got you a present, baby boy."

"What do you mean?" I ask, hardly daring to believe it.

"You have to do a settling-in trial," Benedict says. "But essentially, she's yours. I adopted her for you."

I can't help it. All the emotion I've been pushing down over the past several weeks comes leaking out. I make a sort of keening noise as I turn and bury my face against Benedict's chest, my eyes damp and my throat tight.

"Oh, oh," I whimper, my mind whirring. "But I can't keep her in that tiny dorm room," I protest. It's not like I don't want her. It's more that I'd be devastated if I discovered I couldn't really keep her, after all.

When I look up, Benedict's still grinning. "That's also part of your surprise. I talked to Bobbi about passing this flat on to you after I leave. If you'd be interested?"

My jaw drops open. I know this place is offered at a discounted rate for faculty members. I didn't think TAs usually got anything like this. That's why I'm in the dorm. But if my godmother and my lover want to pull some strings to make an exception, I'm really not going to complain.

The idea of living here without Benedict hurts immediately, though. But if I stayed here just a little while to get on my feet before moving somewhere else, and it would mean I could keep Lizzie…

"I'd be very interested," I whisper. "Oh, Daddy. Are you serious? You're really giving me a cat *and* an apartment?"

He chuckles. "Well, I'd be paving the way for you to rent the apartment yourself at a reduced rate, yes. But also, yes. Lizzie is my gift to you."

A *parting* gift, I know. But that doesn't make it any less

special. In fact, the idea that I'd get to keep her would be like keeping a little part of Daddy with me once he's gone.

"I've been so worried she'd get a good home," I say, wiping the tears from my cheeks and letting Benedict go so I can move carefully toward her. "She's so timid. But she always seemed to like me."

"I know," he says softly. "The clip you sent me was very moving." I make a mental note to buy Selena a very big bunch of flowers for taking that video. "I couldn't get the idea out of my head. So I went to the café to talk to the owner." He shakes his head and rubs the back of his neck. "That Nim is quite the grump, but he cares deeply about finding the cats their forever homes. I told him you'd absolutely cherish her."

I sniff and laugh wetly. "Oh, I'll spoil the shit out of her," I say, making him laugh.

I'm close enough that I can reach my hand out for her to sniff my fingers. She inspects them for a few moments before rubbing her face against them, a purr rumbling from her chest. My heart melts. There's nothing quite like being blessed by a cat with their affection.

"I love that she's called Lizzie," I say, carefully scratching the back of her head. "Like Lizzie Bennet from Pride and Prejudice."

Benedict laughs again and comes over to us, slowly so as not to startle the cat. I now know why Dotty has been shut in the bedroom, so both animals can ease into meeting each other.

"When Bobbi first told me she was giving me you as a TA, I was less than impressed," Benedict says sheepishly. "I thought you were going to be awful."

"What?" I cry, not too loudly so it doesn't startle Lizzie. "Why?"

He crinkles his nose adorably. "Come on. You've got to

admit that 'Jackson Riggs' sounds like a terrible dude bro name."

I have to reluctantly agree. "Yeah, yeah," I grumble. "Why do you think I kept the whole lingerie thing under wraps for so long."

He slips his arm around my waist again. "Precisely. It turned out I was completely wrong, and you were completely lovely. Anyway, the point of the story was that Bobbi told me to wind my pride and prejudice back in. When I discovered the cat you were besotted with was called Lizzie, it seemed like some kind of sign. Fate. I had to make sure you two found each other. Ensuring the flat is passed to you was key in getting the adoption approved."

"Wow," I say softly, then a memory hits me. "Oh my god. Selena used to tease me and call you my very own Mr. Darcy. How crazy is that?"

Benedict grins, apparently not affronted by the comparison to one of literature's grumpiest heroes. "See? Fate. So you definitely want to keep her?"

I huff. "You'd have to fight me to take her back," I say, emotion catching in my voice. "Thank you, Daddy. I mean it."

He kisses me noisily, beaming widely. "Congratulations! You are now also a daddy."

I hum and lean into him as Lizzie's eyes start to close. That means she's starting to trust me, and my already battered heart swells. "A daddy with a little d, though," I say warmly. "You're Daddy with the big D, still."

He snorts. "It is quite big, I suppose," he muses. "But yours is pretty substantial, too."

I laugh and shove against him. "Naughty Daddy."

"Always," he says, then kisses the top of my head. "I'm so happy you like her. She can stay here for now, or you can bring her back to your dorm temporarily if you don't want to be separated. She has a carrier, and I got a couple of litter boxes and bowls and food and such."

I nod. "I think I want to keep her with me," I say. "Thank you, Daddy. I love her so very much."

"You're welcome, baby boy," he says warmly.

My heart might break once he leaves. In fact, I'm sure it will. But at least now, I won't be alone when he's gone.

That's something, at least.

CHAPTER 18

Benedict

The flat is echoey.

I look around at all my stuff packed into brown cardboard boxes. The furniture is staying, as that's all part of the rental, but still, taking all my stuff down has changed the acoustics dramatically.

The flat wasn't as bad as stripping down my office at the college. That went so fast from my little personal oasis here in America to a sad, empty room. Those boxes are still there, piled up and waiting to be collected. I've given Bobbi all my potted plants, and she's promised to do her best not to kill them, but I don't have much hope, to be honest. I guess it's slightly better than just giving up on them and throwing them into the bin, though.

Dotty's lying by my feet, her tail occasionally wagging sadly. I keep telling her we're going home, but I think that's confusing her even more. I hope she'll remember Oxford once we're back there, but her doggy memory has probably long forgotten all about it now.

I hear the key in the lock, and my heart jumps guiltily. It's not difficult to figure out why. Jackson insisted on helping me pack and has really put on a brave face, but god fucking damn it, I don't want to leave him. I keep firmly reminding myself that he's young and he needs to move on and date other guys. If I were to take a gamble and stay, it would put far too much pressure on him.

It was so much easier to tell myself that before I started packing my life away.

No, that's not true. My life is packed away *in Oxford*. When I think of the couple of decades' worth of possessions waiting for me there, it helps remind me that I'm doing the right thing.

Paddle Creek was only ever a pit stop. It's time to start the engine again and get moving. No matter how much it hurts.

"Hey," he says as he comes into the living room. He looks around with wide eyes. "Wow. You're really all done."

I shrug. "There wasn't loads to pack in the end. I'm just taking a carry-on with me on the plane. Then the rest is being picked up next week to ship over with a specialist transatlantic company."

"Yeah, Bobbi mentioned that," Jackson says with a nod.

I pull out the couple of keys from my pocket and fiddle with them. "Are you okay with that? Bobbi's handling every-thing, but technically…" I take a deep breath and hold out the bunch. "I guess it's your place now."

He gives me a smile that doesn't quite meet his eyes. "I guess it is," he agrees as he takes them from me.

It's crazy, but even after all this time, feeling his skin brush against mine still sends such a shiver down my spine. I don't think he'll ever not mesmerize and delight me.

Even when he's no longer mine.

He clears his throat and slips the keys into his pocket. "So your flight's first thing in the morning?"

He knows this, but I don't mind him asking at all. "Yeah," I say with a nod. "Bobbi's taking me. I'm leaving the car here, and someone's picking it up in a day or two." There's a pause where we just look at each other, both putting on a brave face. "Do you want to stay the night?"

"Oh, god, yes," he says with a relieved laugh.

I wrap my arms around him, questioning my decision for the thousandth time. No one's making me leave. I'm doing this voluntarily. I'm honestly not sure if it's the right thing to do or not, but after the last few years of upheaval and uncertainty, I feel it's important to stick to the plan.

Back in Oxford, I'll be able to get a clear head. I know my feelings for this young man are real and strong, and I'm sure they'll stay with me for a long time. But I need to remember who I was before my mother's illness brought me to a place that was her home, not mine.

The trouble is, I don't remember who I was before Jackson, and that seems dangerous. Like I can't trust myself to do the right thing, and as a Dom and a Daddy that's my most important job. I have to look out for Jackson, even if it means making tough decisions and hurting us both in the short term.

He's strong, and I can see him blossoming as a person almost daily since we started this relationship. He's figuring out who he is as well, and it's remarkable. It kills me to think of him being with someone else, but I have faith that he'll be better now at not settling for the kinds of wankers he's hinted at dating in the past.

"Let me cook you dinner," I suggest, rubbing his back and feeling his heart beating against mine.

"I'd love that."

I specifically kept a selection of kitchen things out, as I hoped this was how we could spend the evening. I'm going to make us a butter chicken recipe that my father learned from my grandmother. I cheated and made some vegetable samosas earlier that we snack on, dipping them in cucumber yogurt as we chat and I cook. I've been saving a nice bottle of chianti that we share, and Dotty sits by Jackson's feet where he's sitting at the table. I've got a chilled lofi playlist on quietly in the background.

If it wasn't for all the packed boxes, this would be a perfect picture of domesticity.

We keep our conversations light, mostly talking about students who have graduated. I must say, I'm proud of all of them, as always, but it was especially rewarding to see my two football stars, Seth and Marty, completely turn their grades around. I thought neither of them cared about their studies—only football. It was wonderful to be proved wrong, and I know their other boyfriend, Gabe, played a huge part in that.

I'm sorry to be leaving our transfer student, Xander Patterson, halfway through his masters. He was incredibly stressed and overloaded at the start of the year when he came into my class. I think he was trying to juggle a crappy job with his studies as well. But something seems to be improving for him, and Bobbi and the rest of my staff have promised to keep an eye out for him.

Jackson's going to be transferring himself to the dean's office. Apparently, his work for me this year has impressed the right people, and he's actually going to be moving back into an executive assistant role, just with proper pay this time. No more interning for free for my boy.

My boy. I wonder how long I'll think of him like that. Possibly forever. I've never had a boy before, and I'm not sure I will again. Being a Dom is in my nature. But I don't think I could be anyone else's Daddy. I've loved it more than words, but that was something special Jackson and I shared. I don't think I could do that for anyone else, even though I'll miss caring for someone so intimately. The control he gave me—the trust he put in me—was the kind of reward I've never felt anywhere else. I don't imagine I will again.

There's no leaving the washing-up till the morning tonight, and it seems silly to run the dishwasher for so few things. So Jackson and I stand at the sink. I wash while he dries, then we put it all away for him to inherit. I have my own crockery back in storage, and he doesn't have these kinds of things, as he hasn't been living with a kitchen.

It feels so incredibly strange to think of him here without me. Right now, it hurts, but I hope sometime in the not-too-distant future, it will bring me comfort.

The mood shifts as the heavy weight of inevitability settles over us. I'm sure neither of us are tired, but we go to bed early regardless as anything else felt kind of like torture. We make love slowly, no games. Just Daddy and his baby boy. I move deep inside him, savoring every last moment that I get to call him mine.

I don't sleep much, but that's okay. It means I get to watch him breathe. I study the sharp lines of his jaw and the soft lashes that feather on the tops of his cheeks.

He's wearing the leather string necklace, and I wonder if he'll put the collar we bought him on again when I'm gone. I'm happy he's keeping it. Like with Lizzie, the cat, I wanted to leave some mementos behind so a part of me can almost stay with him. But a selfish part of me hopes that he won't play with that collar with anyone else.

We've only taken a few photos together. My favorite was one particularly glorious day out walking Dotty. I know I'll be looking at that photo a lot in the coming months. But I want to remember how I feel with him right now, in this moment. How solid and real he is in my arms.

Because when the morning comes, I'll drop him off at his dorm like I have a hundred times before. Then I'll return to this flat and wait for Bobbi to take Dotty and me to the airport, then that will be it.

The chapter of my life that was Paddle Creek will be over.

Jackson and I will be over.

I hate it, but I guess that's the way it's got to be. I'll survive, and I know he'll thrive. We'll be okay. I hope.

In the gloom of the night, I look over toward the closed blinds of the window. It's always darkest before the dawn.

I just wonder how long this darkness will last.

CHAPTER 19

Jackson

"Go away!" I mumble from under my duvet. The banging on my door scared Lizzie off to her new favorite hiding spot between my dresser and the wall. Cuddling her was the only thing stopping me from losing it completely.

Of course the thumping doesn't stop.

"Jackson Travis Riggs, you get your butt out of that bed and you open this door right now!" Selena yells. I cringe. It's Saturday morning. I know a lot of students will have gone home, but some might still be around nursing hangovers. It doesn't matter how many of them kept me up with parties. I can't take any more stress this morning.

"Shh!" I plead with my best friend, but she just keeps pounding.

I sigh, grab a tissue to wipe my eyes and blow my nose, then drag myself out of bed to unlock the door.

The second it's open, she barges in and throws her arms around me. "It's okay. I'm here."

"I noticed," I grumble.

She huffs, then holds me by my shoulders, studying my

face. Then she kicks the door shut again and drags me over to sit on the bed. "So he's gone."

I shrug. "He's probably only just leaving for Fort Wayne," I say, glancing at the clock on my desk. "He's connecting at O'Hare before heading to Heathrow."

"I don't care if he's in London or Chicago or Timbuktu!" Selena cries. "You didn't do it, did you?"

"Upset us both even more before he leaves?" I quip with just a little rancor.

She throws up her hands. "Tell him you love him and *beg* him to stay!"

"I told you—"

Real anger flashes over her face.

"You're really going to let the best man you ever dated walk away because you were too chicken shit to tell him how important he is to you? Both of you are morons! I don't know what's going on in his head, but the fact that you haven't had a hard, long talk about this tells me that you're both so concerned about upsetting the other that you'd rather break both your hearts!"

I open and close my mouth, but I'm feeling so wretched right now, I can't really argue with her. I was so scared of being flat out rejected by Benedict that I kept the depth of my feelings hidden and secret. But could that conversation have made me feel any worse than I do right now?

I feel myself crumbling. My eyes burn, and my throat thickens. "He's really gone," I manage to whisper.

I know it's utterly crazy, but in that moment, it hits me like a ton of bricks. I actually might never see him again. And I missed every opportunity to tell him that I love him.

"I'm a fucking idiot," I whimper.

Selena gently cups her hands on either side of my face. "Yes, you are," she says firmly. "If you weren't honest with him, how would he know there was anything truly worth staying for?"

I stare at her as the horror creeps through me. "I've made a terrible mistake," I rasp. "Oh, god. I love him. I love him *so much.* I can't just let him slip away! I should have fought for him! I *have* to fight for him! Selena!"

She's already thrusting my phone into my hands. "Better late than never, I suppose," she mutters. "Call him. Get him to turn around. You still have time to talk face-to-face."

My hands are trembling, but I quickly pull up his details and hit the button.

Straight to voicemail.

I try again, but it's the same result. And a third time. Before I can try again, Selena grabs my wrist and shakes her head. "Fuck it. You're sure he'll have left by now?"

I look at the clock. His flight is at half past twelve. Bobbi was supposed to be picking him up at ten, and it's five past now. My godmother is never late. If anything, she'll have been there twenty minutes early, hustling him along.

"Yeah," I say, defeat washing over me.

But Selena is still grinning. She lunges over to my desk, then shoves something else into my hands.

My car keys.

"If you go right now, you can stop him before he gets through security."

My eyebrows shoot up. "You think I should drive to Fort Wayne?"

She glares. "Don't make me use your full name again," she growls. "You've been ignoring me for weeks. You're an idiot, remember? But I love you, so, yes. You're going to run to your car right now, jump on the highway, and beat him to the metal detectors. You've got nothing to lose!"

I swallow and look between my keys and then over at

Lizzie's sweet face which is looking hopefully out at me. My love for her reminds me just what I'm fighting for.

"I'm going to go get my Daddy," I say breathlessly, my heart pounding and my body shaking. I jump to my feet, and my best friend does the same. "I've been a complete moron but it's not over yet!"

"Not until the fat lady sings!" Selena cries, punching the air. She spins around, snatching up my wallet before grabbing my sneakers. "Now go! I'll look after Lizzie! You've got this! Tell him how you feel, and then you know you'll have done everything you can!"

I throw my arms around her and kiss her cheek noisily. "Never stop being right about everything," I say, half laughing, half crying.

She smacks my arm. "Thank me later! More running now!"

I shove my feet into my shoes and tear out the door.

I'm going to get my man.

———

Or…not.

I stand in front of my smoking car, the hood up by the side of the road, without a clue what to do. I've tried calling Benedict again, but it's still going straight to voicemail.

I never even made it out of Paddle Creek.

I drag my hands through my hair and let out a guttural scream up to the sky, regretting so many life choices that brought me to this moment. First and foremost, buying such a crappy car.

That's it. If Benedict's phone is off, then he might as well be back in Oxford already. It's over.

I can't help it. I turn away from the busy road and hug myself as I start to cry. I'm so *angry* at myself. I was so wrapped up in doing the right thing and respecting Benedict's wishes that I wasn't honest with him. Selena's right. I thought because he didn't make some big declaration that he didn't want me anymore. But that goes two ways. Why would he change the plan he's had for years unless I gave him a reason to? I should have shouted from the rooftops and written it in the sky that I'm madly in love with him and can't imagine my life without him.

And now everything is ruined.

I was a coward to hide away the parts of me that made me the happiest until Benedict came along. But I was still a coward when it mattered the most. I let him go, and even if we keep talking once he turns his phone back on in the UK, chances are I've already lost him forever.

"Hey, buddy? Are you okay?"

I jolt from my miserable reverie to see a guy has pulled over in a pickup truck. I suppose the traffic on the road is loud, but I was so consumed in my despair that I didn't even notice him approach.

He's a solid guy, and I'd guess he'd be in his mid-to-late forties. His lumberjack shirt hugs his big torso, and his jeans look well worn. An auburn beard covers the lower half of his face, but his mouth is crooked in a half smile, and he's holding his hands up like he doesn't want to spook me.

My immediate response is relief. He seems kind. That's probably how most serial killers operate, but fuck it. I'm pretty much at rock bottom right now and I'm not going to smack away a friendly offer.

I take a shuddery breath and hastily rub the tears from my cheeks as best I can. "I have to get to the airport," I say pitifully. "But my car started making a funny noise and smoking under the hood, so I pulled off the road, but now it won't start at all."

The guy nods. "You did the right thing. My name's Ruben. I'm a mechanic. You mind if I take a look?"

The laugh that escapes my throat is a little desperate. "Please, be my guest!" I cry. I anxiously check my watch, wondering how much time I have.

Ruben tips his baseball cap at me, calm warmth radiating from his persona. He bends over to check around my engine, poking a few things.

"Okay," he says after only a minute or so. "Have you never changed your air filter, kid? Don't answer that, obviously you haven't." He chuckles to himself and I cringe sheepishly in agreement. "As long as that's the worst of it, it shouldn't take that long to fix."

Relief washes through me. "Really?"

But Ruben grimaces as he straightens up from the car and brushes his hands together. "Sorry, kid. I don't have one this size on me. We can tow it back to the garage where I should have one there, but you said something about catching a plane?"

Of course it wouldn't be that easy.

Grief and anger well up in me again as I shake my head. "I'm trying to reach my boyfriend before he goes through security. He's going back to England, forever. And I'm the *idiot* who didn't tell him I love him or beg him to stay, and now everything's ruined, and I'm going to lose him *forever* and—"

"Whoa!" the big guy waves his hands at me. "Slow down. What time's his flight?"

I check the time on my phone. "Not for another couple of hours."

Ruben nods. "So there's a chance you could still catch him."

I laugh hollowly. "If I clicked my heels three times," I say, thinking of Dotty with another pang of sadness.

"What about driving?" he asks patiently.

I frown. "Yeah, but my car's—"

He snaps his fingers and points at me. "Is there anything you need in your car?"

I blink and take a moment to think. "No, I put everything in my pockets."

"Great." He claps his large hands together. "Lock her up and get in."

"G-get in?" I splutter, not understanding but locking it anyway. Ruben has pulled out his cell phone from his jeans and presses it to his ear.

"Yeah, kid. We're going to the airport. Lewis! We've got a tow out north on the interstate. I'm with the passenger. It needs a new air filter. Can you come out and get her lickety-split?" He nods as he pulls a reflective hazard warning sign out of the truck bed and drops it behind my car. "Fantastic. You're the man." He closes the call and marches over to the driver's side of the truck. "Come on, kid! Is it true love or what?"

I come comically back to life, scrabbling on the dirt as I flail my arms and run over to the passenger side. "Oh, it's true love, all right," I cry giddily.

"Good boy," he tells me with a wink as I jam my seat belt on. I know he's not my Daddy, but those words still soothe me immeasurably.

He pulls out into the traffic like a bat out of hell. Country rock blares out of his speakers, and a Hawaiian dancer jiggles from the rearview mirror. I grip onto the cracked leather seat, my heart racing as Ruben really floors it, considering we're in an old Ford F-150 and not a Ferrari.

"So, you're an idiot, huh?" he quips over the music, but his eyes crinkle as he glances over at me, showing that kindness again.

"Yeah," I say with a shaky laugh. "My best friend's been telling me for months."

"It's okay," Ruben says, expertly changing lanes. "Love makes idiots out of all of us."

There's something about his tone that makes me feel like he's speaking from experience, but he doesn't elaborate further.

"Tell me about him," he asks instead, and my insides instantly glow with warmth.

I haven't been able to talk to anyone about Benedict aside from Selena, and to be honest, those conversations have been blighted for the last several weeks by her insistence I grow up and talk to him and my stubbornness to rock the boat. Not to mention that we've had to be so careful and keep everything secret. Talking to a stranger suddenly feels like a kind of therapy.

"He's…everything," I say, shaking my head. I'm still not going to use his name, just in case, but I can talk about other things. "He's kind and caring but also commanding. Handsome. My god, the way he wears a suit. He's always thinking of others. He makes me feel so special. He's a great cook and has the most gorgeous dog. Oh! And he adopted a cat for me!"

Ruben chuckles. "And why exactly is he heading to England forever?"

"He's British," I say dejectedly. "He was only in Paddle Creek to look after his mom. She passed away last year. The plan was always to go home, and I stuck to that because apparently the stupid plan was more important than being honest about my feelings."

He laughs again. "Do you think he feels the same way?"

I shrug. "That's what I'm rushing to the airport to find out."

"Okay, then." Ruben manages to make the truck go just a little faster.

It feels like it takes forever to get to the airport, but in reality, we don't hit any traffic by some miracle, and Ruben screeches to a halt outside the passenger drop off zone.

"I'll wait in the short stay lot," he tells me as I'm yanking my seat belt off and scrabbling at the car door. He grabs a business card from a box in a little cubby hold. "Hey, kid. Call me, and I'll drive you home, okay? No matter what happens."

I try and swallow down my emotions as I take it. "You've been a literal angel, Ruben," I say. "Thank you. I'm Jackson, by the way."

"Good luck, Jackson," he says sagely. "Now, run like the wind!"

I don't need telling twice. I jump out of the truck and slam the door, dashing between the other waiting cars and rushing into the main entrance of Fort Wayne. I haven't been here a whole lot, as I never really fly for vacations. I'm more of a camping kind of guy. So it takes me a few moments to work out where I should even look. Then I spot an electronic board with destinations written on it, and realize there are check-in desks by the different airline companies.

"O'Hare, O'Hare," I mutter frantically, scanning down until I find the right time. "Bingo!" Counter ten. That's to my right, so I break into a sprint, my heart in my throat. I'm frantically checking every face I see before I even get there. When I see the line and push my legs even harder, I look up and down the snake of passengers, trying to find Benedict.

He's not there.

Okay—two options. I somehow beat him here, or he's already gone through. If I beat him, I can camp out at the coffee shop behind me and wait. But if he's already checked in…

I look around for the signs to security. *Fuck.* It looks like you can go either left or right from here. I have to gamble.

I choose right. It looks slightly closer.

"Excuse me! Thank you!" I say over and over as I weave through people at a sprint as if I'm a quarterback aiming for a touchdown. I vault over a little kid's ride-on case like I'm in the hundred-meter hurdles at the Olympics. Thank fuck I'm always at the gym because even so my legs are starting to protest at the sudden relentless burst of activity.

I dash past the tables where you have to bag up your liquids and get rid of any drinks. Security is mostly hidden through an archway for logical reasons, but I'm still desperately searching for that one familiar face.

In the end, it's four familiar little legs I recognize.

I grind to a halt and gasp. There he is. Benedict is getting Dotty out of her carrier so they can walk through the metal detectors. His suitcase is already going through the belt. He's beyond where he scanned his passport, so I can't reach him. I don't know what else to do.

But I can't let him go now.

"BENEDICT!" I bellow at the top of my lungs, my hands balled into fists.

A hundred people must turn and look at me. An eerie still falls around the area. But Benedict doesn't look. Didn't he hear me? I don't think I could be any louder.

A security officer approaches me, his hand raised. "Is there a problem here, sir?"

I almost scoff. *I'm* not 'Sir.'

"No, I just…my boyfriend…" My eyes are trained desperately on Benedict as he picks Dotty up, then I can just about see him frown as he looks around. I think he realizes other people have stilled.

And then he turns his gaze in the same direction as everyone else.

My heart leaps, and I wave frantically. His jaw drops. I don't blame him. This is insane.

"Sir," the security guard says in a warning tone, but I point excitedly.

"That's my boyfriend! It's an emergency. I promise everything's okay."

The guard frowns but steps away as I rush forward to the I.D. checkpoint. I keep my gaze glued to Benedict as he looks between me and his suitcase which has already gone through the X-ray machine.

"I'm so sorry," he says to the attendant by the belt. "I just have to…I'll be back for my case. Hang on."

He places Dotty back on the floor, then the two of them jog back along the line of passengers, almost all of them watching him or staring at me. I don't care. He's here. I caught him in the nick of time.

I hold my breath as he comes back to the checkpoint. The guy at the desk is narrowing his eyes at us. Benedict flashes his passport. "I don't suppose I could just nip back over, could I?"

The guy thinks about it for a moment but then huffs and manually opens the gate for Benedict to dash through.

"Jackson?" he cries in disbelief as he throws his arms around me. Dotty barks a few times and runs around my legs, catching me in her leash. "What is it? What's wrong?"

"Everything," I choke out, gripping onto his shoulders. "I should have said something weeks ago. I…Benedict, I love you. I know you have to get on a plane, but I don't want this relationship to end. I can't let it! I've been a complete fool and a coward, but you taught me to be brave, and Selena smacked the stupidity out of me. So I'm here, now, begging you not to give up on us, to give this a chance. I know the Atlantic is a big fucking ocean, but I—"

His mouth crashes into mine, swallowing up my last-ditch attempt not to lose the love of my life.

After a few passionate moments, he pulls back. "You love me?" he asks breathlessly.

I nod. "I know that's not a fair thing to confess as you're about to get on a plane, but—"

"Stop talking," he cries with a laugh, kissing me again. "That's all you had to say."

"It was?"

He grins, ignoring the sea of onlookers around us. "I love you, too, baby boy."

Maybe my life isn't over, after all.

CHAPTER 20

Benedict

"You love me?" Jackson repeats. I feel almost delirious. I'm not even sure what's happening, but I know that he's here in my arms and he loves me.

My boy loves me.

Oh, I've been such a fool.

What seemed so right and certain is all crumbling away in this moment of clarity I'm seeing before me. I've been so dead set on returning to my old life that I never allowed myself to really think if it'll even be *there* for me when I return. Things have changed. I've changed.

Jackson is right here, and he loves me.

The security guard is glaring at us, and people are slowing up the security checks because they're too busy trying to get a look at us. Sorry, folks. This is a private show. I steer Jackson around the corner to where we're not being gawked at so much.

"I love you with my whole heart," I say, shaking my head. "More than words can possibly say. But you're so young. You deserve the chance to spread your wings and to see other people."

He looks at me warily. "Do you *want* me to see other people?"

I'm standing on one side of passport control, and my suitcase is on the other. My plane leaves in just over an hour. It's time to stop beating about the bush and be bloody honest for once.

"No," I say firmly. "But—"

"But nothing!" Jackson cries. He shakes his hands in frustration, but he's also laughing. "Oh my god. Is that why you pushed me away? You decided I needed to play the field some more?"

"I didn't push you away," I mumble.

He indicates the security gate. "What do you call flying to London?"

"Fair point," I say with a lopsided grin. "I was just trying to do what was best for you."

He sighs and shakes his head. "And I let you. I was trying to respect your wishes. I thought you didn't care about me enough to discuss another option. But if you thought you were doing me a favor, that's bullshit."

"Jackson—"

"No," he snaps, jabbing a finger at me. "Selena was right. We've both been complete idiots about this! I don't want anyone else but you, Benedict! I love *you!* And I know you're Daddy and you take care of me, but if you thought you were doing what was best for me, I'm sorry, but in this case you were so wrong."

I drop Dotty's lead and stand on the end, freeing up both my hands to cup either side of his face. We look into each other's eyes.

"I'm sorry," I say eventually. "You're right. I thought I was doing what was best for you, but we should have talked instead of making all these assumptions."

"It's okay," he says with a sad sigh. "I just couldn't let you leave without finally telling you the truth. Without fighting to keep…something going between us."

"I can't believe you came all the way to the airport," I say incredulously, my heart so full. I should never have doubted the seriousness of this relationship. I was too afraid of it to see how bloody strong it is despite both our best efforts to diminish its importance.

Jackson laughs hollowly and shakes his head in my hands. "I had to come here! Your phone is switched off! I did try and call you several times before I made a mad dash across the state."

I frown. My phone isn't off, is it? I let him go to get it out of my pocket and groan. "I must have already put it on airplane mode. I don't even remember doing that." I suspect I was so miserable about leaving Jackson behind I was already shutting everything out, perhaps even subconsciously. "Oh, baby boy. I'm so sorry. You must have been so stressed."

It's his turn to cup the side of my face, rubbing the stubble with his thumb. "It's okay. I had some help. And I made it here in time, didn't I?" He looks behind me at the security gate. "I suppose you have to go now," he says heavily.

I blink and laugh. "I guess I should rescue my suitcase and Dotty's carrier, yeah."

He swallows and steps away from me. "Yeah. Well…will you let me know when you get to Chicago?"

I give him a curious look. "Chicago?"

He nods. "If that's okay. I'd like to keep talking. Work out where we stand and what we want to do. You don't have to say anything much, just that you've landed and you're safe. We can talk more when you get back to England. I mean, if that's what you want. It's, um, what I want."

I see we've missed a step here. I shake my head and hold on to his shoulders. "I don't need time to think about anything. I know exactly what I want. I'm not getting on that plane. I'm staying right here."

His beautiful blue eyes go impossibly large. "W-what?"

He was right. I messed up royally by not trusting him to talk this through like adults. But I'm done dancing around the issue and making decisions for him based on fear.

"If I stayed in Paddle Creek," I say plainly, "would you still want to keep seeing each other?"

He just stares at me for a moment. "Are you kidding me? What kind of question is that? *Yes!* Of course I'd want to keep seeing each other! But..." He chews his lip and shakes his head. "I wouldn't want to keep hiding. I know I still technically work for the university, but not you. I'd want to be out and proud. I'd want to be all in as a couple."

My heart contracts, and I seriously think about what he's saying.

I'm sad to say that my knee-jerk reaction is fear. I've spent so long hiding who I am. My true nature. My deepest desires. But it's Jackson who's helped me to see that I've got nothing to be ashamed of. And it's not like we'd be parading what we do for all to know. He's talking about being boyfriends for the world to see.

And when I think about it like that, there's no one I'd be prouder to have by my side in life.

"That depends," I say, unable to resist teasing him a little in this important moment. "Are you going to tell your godmother I'm shagging you senseless, or do I have to?"

It takes him a second to catch on to what I'm saying, then he gasps. "Are you serious? Is that a yes? You want to date and be out and everything?"

I wrap my arms around him, feeling like the weight of the world has been lifted from my shoulders. "A thousand percent yes, baby boy. I feel like you've just pulled me back from jumping off a cliff and making the worst mistake of my life. I am absolutely all in."

He kisses me so hard there's a danger of us both falling over. Dotty yaps, and we stop with a laugh, which is probably for the best, considering the way the security guard is glaring at us. Fuck him. I'm the happiest man alive right now.

Jackson groans. "Oh, but what about your flight?"

I shrug. "I'll tell them I don't need it anymore. Maybe I'll get a refund, but honestly, I don't care." I rub his back and kiss him sweetly again. "You're more important than money."

"I am?"

I shake my head. "If you even have to ask that, I really have been a terrible Daddy," I lament.

He laughs and buries his face against my neck. "You're the best Daddy in the whole world," he says sincerely.

"I'm going to spend every day trying to earn that title," I promise.

He leans back and waggles his eyebrows at me. "Can we start with you taking me home and fucking my brains out?"

I bark out a laugh that definitely gets us a pointed stare from the security guard. "That sounds like a perfect way to start the next chapter of our lives together."

"The *next* chapter," he repeats, his voice thick with emotion. "I like the sound of that."

"Me, too," I agree. "Very much. Oh," I add softly, realization dawning—the good kind. "If I stay…that also means I don't have to leave my mum behind."

He bites his lip, his eyes glassy as he smiles. "I was going to look after her," he says.

I kiss him and hold him tightly as emotions swirl inside me. I said goodbye to my father a long time ago, but I'm glad I don't have to abandon my mother's grave so soon after her parting.

"We can visit her together," I say, my heart swelling at the thought. I'm going to hold my baby boy's hand and tell my mum he's my boyfriend so if she's looking down on us, she'll know for sure.

Saying that, Jackson's right. I think everyone else realized we were in love and being utter morons long before we did. I bet Mum is cheering me on right now for finally getting my act together, wherever she is.

"Okay, let's go rescue my suitcase before it gets lost forever," I suggest. "Are you okay to drive us home?"

"Actually…we have a ride," Jackson says sheepishly, grinning at me.

"We do?"

He nods. "It's kind of a long story."

I pull him against me and kiss him just because I can. "Luckily, we have all the time in the world for long stories now."

I can't really believe that my whole life has just changed in a matter of minutes, all because I'm lucky enough to have the bravest, most passionate boy in the world. If he thinks he's the lucky one, he's wrong. I am. He hasn't just saved me from getting on that plane. He's saved me from myself and the shame I've been living with for so many years.

In reality, my whole life changed when I walked into that lecture hall and saw him for the very first time. I've tried to fight it, but there's no arguing with destiny, it seems.

Now we don't have to resist anymore. No more secrets. I proudly take his hand, declaring to the world that Jackson Riggs is mine.

Possibly forever.

CHAPTER 21

Jackson

The drive home feels like it takes forever. I'm thankful we have Ruben as our own private chauffeur and that we don't have to mess around with taxis, but it's a kind of torture being pressed up against Benedict's side in the front seat for the whole journey and not being able to touch him the way I want to.

Luckily, Ruben is captivated by Dotty, who sits on Benedict's lap as good as gold for the whole ride. Apparently, Ruben's boyfriend has a dog, but again there's a hint of sadness when he says that. He doesn't elaborate further on that, either, and I wonder what his story is.

"You can pick up your car any time you like today," he informs me cheerfully when we finally get to Benedict's apartment. "She's all ready to go." Then he waggles his eyebrows at Benedict, who's busy getting his suitcase from the back of the truck. "Or you can swing by tomorrow if you're going to be busy the rest of the day."

I can't hide my grin, and the fact I don't have to anymore just makes me even happier.

"Um, yeah," I say, blushing and not caring. "I think we're going to be pretty busy."

"Good boy," Ruben says with a wink. "Catch you later, kid."

I take Dotty's leash as Benedict pulls his case to the front door. I pause to wave good-bye to Ruben before he drives off, and then I use my keys to get inside the building. "I suppose you're going to need your set back from Bobbi," I comment as we head up the stairs.

Benedict pauses on the landing, looking at me seriously. "Would you want to live together?" he asks.

My god, I'm adoring this new way of plain speaking we have. Direct questions with direct answers.

"Yes," I say without hesitation. "I know we've only been together a few months, but it doesn't feel fast to me. It just feels right."

He hugs me right there out in the open. We're really doing this. We're going to be out and proud. No more secrets other than the spicy ones we want to keep between us and the bedroom.

"That would make me incredibly happy, baby boy," he says warmly.

"Actually, Sir," I say, feeling my heart starting to race. We *are* alone, after all. "I think you'll find I've been a very naughty girl. You should definitely take me into your office and teach me a lesson or two."

Heat blazes in his eyes as he leans in closer. "You better be wearing something pretty for me," he murmurs.

I bat my eyelashes at him. "What kind of a filthy slut would I be if I wasn't? You know I'm always desperate for Sir's big, fat cock."

He groans and bites his lip. "On the bed, now. Clothes off. You're going to take that big cock however I decide to give it to you."

My blood is rushing so hard I almost feel faint. God, I thought I'd lost him forever, and now it feels like we've got forever stretching out before us together.

I run up the last flight of stairs, hurriedly letting myself in. The apartment is still filled with boxes, but all that does is remind me that Benedict is really here, that he never left. I leave the door ajar then dash into the bedroom, quickly throwing the bedsheet that we took off this morning back on. I grab a couple of pillows then tear my jeans and hoodie off. I'm only wearing simple blue panties and a bralette, but I don't need anything fancy right now to role-play for my Daddy. I just need him.

He packed the lube, so there isn't really anything else for me to do. I lie on my back with my arms over my head, hoping I look wanton and helpless. I hear him come through the door and a few noises that suggest he's getting Dotty some water and making her comfortable.

I texted Selena to let her know what happened and between all the screaming and happy emojis, she agreed to hang out with Lizzie a little longer. I plan on going to pick her up later. Hell, I plan on moving into the apartment tonight. But right now, Benedict and I need some alone time to heal from the terrible mistake we almost made.

He wore a sweater to the airport, but when he strides through the bedroom door, he's taken the time to put a shirt on and button it up. He's got a folded-up tie clenched in his fist, and he has an air of danger about him as he forcefully shuts the door.

"There you are," he growls.

I gasp, a little spike of adrenaline flashing through me, telling me to run, to get away.

He's on me before I can do anything, though. He straddles my hips and wraps the tie in a figure of eight around my wrists before attaching it to the bed. It's not the most secure restraint, but that's not the point right now.

The point is I'm his and he can do whatever he wants with me.

He unzips the fly on his pants and pulls out his cock, stroking it leisurely. "Where shall I make you take it first, you naughty girl? I'm going to fuck all that disobedience out of you. That'll teach you to whore yourself around. You're *my* slut. You're here so I can fuck you whenever I want, and *only* me."

I lick my lips, watching as he gets a condom and lube out of his pocket.

I meant it. I'm all in.

"You don't need that, Sir," I say softly, nodding at the shiny foil wrap. "You're right. I'm *your* slut. No one else's. I want you to come inside me and fill me with your hot, salty seed."

Benedict pauses, his character slipping. He puts the condom down on the bed and caresses the side of my face. "Are you sure, pretty girl?"

I nod. "I haven't been with anyone else since you first seduced me. I went to the clinic. I-I want to have your baby."

I know clear communication is important when discussing safe sex, but fuck it. I don't want to break the scene completely, and I watch him carefully to make sure he understands me.

He brushes his thumb against my cheekbone. "You just want time off your studies," he says in a low rumble.

I shake my head. "I think we'd make a beautiful baby."

He leans down and kisses me deeply. Then he bumps our noses together and nips at my lower lip. "It'll probably take a while to impregnate you," he says, his voice low and threatening. "I'd better fuck you a lot to make sure it happens."

"Will you keep me locked up until I'm round with your heir?" I ask.

I know I'm sliding around scenarios, but I don't care, and it doesn't look like Benedict does either. He grinds his hard length against my thigh through his pants and kisses me roughly on the mouth.

"Yes, I think that's sensible. I can't have you running away. Your only purpose in life now is to pleasure me whenever I want it. You're my prisoner, wench."

"You brute!" I cry and pull at the tie around my wrists. "I'll resist you. I'll never be yours!"

He hums and sucks my neck. "Too late. I already own you. No one's coming to rescue you."

Good. That's just the way I want it.

I gasp as he suddenly seizes my hips and drags my panties down my legs. They're not the kind with the easy access hole in the back—I really wasn't expecting to have sex today, after all. But I love being almost completely naked while he's fully clothed, towering over me. By keeping the bra on, I still feel feminine. It's perfect.

He hoists my ankles over his shoulders and thrusts a lubricated finger inside my boy pussy. I cry out and clench my muscles around the digit, our gazes locked as he begins to take me.

"You like that, don't you, you little slut?" he murmurs, quickly adding another finger. My cock bounces against my stomach, dripping precum.

"I love it," I whimper, turning my head away. "I shouldn't want you, but I do, Sir."

"I know," he says with savage glee. "It was only a matter of time before you submitted. You belong on your knees, sucking my cock."

"Oh, please, *please*," I beg.

He removes his fingers and uses his dry hand to force my

head to turn and look at him again as he crawls up the bed. "Is this what you want?" he asks, roughly rubbing the swollen tip of his dick against my lips.

"Yes, Sir," I hiss.

He pushes inside my mouth, making me choke and gag as he thrusts deep into my throat. He drops his head back in ecstasy as I swallow him down eagerly, blinking away the tears that spring into my eyes. They run down the side of my face onto the pillow. I pull at my restraints, showing him I'm still at his mercy. I wish my ankles were tied up as well.

Later. We have all the time in the world now.

He doesn't fuck my face for long. When he stops, he moves so he can lean down and claim my mouth with his, thrusting his tongue inside like he did his cock. "Good girl," he murmurs. "So good for your master."

"Fuck me, Sir, please," I whine. "I need you inside me. I need your seed."

He kisses me once more, then moves back down the bed, hoisting up my feet again. He hasn't stretched me much, but that's what I want. I need to feel him. He douses his naked cock in lube and pours plenty along my crack as well. Then he angles himself up and wastes no time in pushing the tip around my tight hole.

"Good girl," he pants as I try not to squirm too much and accept him. "That's it, good girl. Take it for Daddy."

"Daddy," I say, practically sobbing. "Daddy, I love you. Please take me. I'm yours. Take me. Touch me. *Fuck* me."

"Good boy," he says this time, forcing his way farther in. It burns but it feels incredible. "I love you, too. Such a good, pretty boy for Daddy. You can take all of his big cock, can't you? You love getting fucked in your tight little pussy by Daddy."

I squeal and jut my hips up to meet him. This is everything I want and more. This is my life now.

I'm the luckiest boy—who's sometimes a girl—in the world.

"Daddy, Daddy, Daddy," I repeat as he starts to fuck me in earnest. He knows the exact angle how to hit my prostate, lighting me up from within. Neither of us are going to last long, it's obvious, so I'm relieved when he takes my neglected cock in hand and starts jerking me off.

"Come for me, baby boy. Come for Daddy. Show me you're mine."

It only takes a few more strokes until I'm spurting all over myself, howling in ecstasy. Even through my high, I feel him start to throb and come within me. This time, there's nothing at all between us. I take everything he gives me greedily with a full and happy heart.

He unhooks my legs, then drops on top of me, hugging me tightly to him.

"Oh, baby," he says, sounding exhausted but happy. I know the feeling.

For a while, we just cling to each other. A few tears escape my eyes, but they're from relief more than anything else. I've been so worried for so long, and now I've been set free. Of all the scenarios I've been imagining for my future over the past few months, this is the best possible one. The one I never even dared dream of because it seemed so impossible.

Benedict is going to stay. We're going to start our lives together as a real couple. We're going to share a bed and make love and role-play whenever we want to.

What did I do in a past life to deserve such bliss?

There's one last puzzle piece I want to slot into place, and now feels like the right time to do so.

"I think I'm genderfluid," I say out of the blue. Of course Benedict just looks up from where his head was resting on the pillow beside mine and smiles down at me.

"That sounds good to me," he says warmly. "Labels can really help us feel at home in our own skins."

I nod, feeling an extra bonus relief. I've come out as gay. I came out with my lingerie. And now I'm coming out with my gender identity. It makes me feel whole.

"They have a pretty flag, too," I say playfully.

He grins and kisses me sweetly. "A pretty flag for a pretty boy."

"Maybe now that you're staying we can go to Indianapolis Pride together this summer?" I suggest. Fuck, it feels *amazing* to be able to make plans with him. I don't think I truly appreciated how much the end date of our relationship was really weighing down on me. I told myself it gave us freedom because there wasn't another option. I was trying to make the best out of the situation.

I prefer the actual freedom of a future together much more.

"I'd love to, baby boy," he says.

I want to plan everything now. Vacations. Thanksgiving and Christmas. I want him to meet my family. We're going to live together. This is just the beginning.

I can't wait for what's to come.

Epilogue

ONE YEAR LATER – BENEDICT

Wow. Jackson really went all out on this one. I hoped he would, but still.

I've walked into our bedroom in the apartment to find him sitting on the mattress like usual. I asked him not to try and restrain himself this time, but to have fun with set dressing if he wanted.

Apparently, he wanted to very much.

He's got a bunch of white fairy lights out from the Christmas decorations and wound them around the bed frame. They illuminate the darkened room along with the bedside lamps, giving the scene a warm, intimate glow. Also wrapped around the slats of the headboard are trails of artificial roses, and there are red petals strewn over the duvet around his legs. A fresh pine incense stick is burning on the dresser, filling the air with a subtle foresty scent. His phone is playing quiet background music of wind chimes and other soothing sounds.

But of course it's him who's stealing the scene. When I asked for a kidnapped bride, I thought he'd re-purpose the toga he's used for so many scenes before. But he's managed to source a lightweight white dress with an off-the-shoulder sweetheart neck, fitted waist, and a fabulous dip hem skirt that billows out under his legs down to his feet, but it's short enough at the front for me to be able to see the matching frilly garters he's wearing. My mouth waters, imagining what underwear I can't see, but that's for later.

He's even got a veil that's attached to a glittering tiara on his head, the gauzy fabric pushed back so I can see his face. His makeup skills have really improved over this last year as he's gotten more confident wearing it in everyday life. His skin looks so smooth, his lips and eyes dazzle, and the high-lighter on his cheekbones shines.

For a second, I marvel at how far he's come since we first met. He's perfectly happy wearing skirts and lip gloss to work now. It helps that his godmother would probably fire anyone who dared have a problem with it. She almost fired *me* when we told her we were dating, but thankfully she calmed down and saw how happy we are, giving me that pay rise instead.

Everybody won. But mostly me, I think.

Around Jackson's neck is the silver necklace I bought him for Christmas with a diamond pendant that sits just below his throat. I know he wears it every day—and we often scene with his collar or one of my ties—but I never get tired of seeing something of mine around his neck, reminding us both that he belongs to me.

It's time to put that theory to the test now, though.

It's a long time since I've felt nervous for a scene. Certainly not since Jackson and I started dating after that first vulnerable encounter. I'm the Dom. I'm supposed to be calm, collected, and most of all, in control. But I'm also only human, and damn it if my heart isn't pounding in my chest.

"You wicked brute!" Jackson cries, perfectly in character as usual. "How could you kidnap me on the day of my wedding? You'll never get away with this!" He slaps the mattress petulantly, and a smile tugs at the corner of my lips.

God, I love him so much.

My costumes are never as elaborate as his, but a while back, we invested in a white billowy shirt that serves very well as a hunter ravishing a wood nymph or a pirate with his mermaid or nobleman in a state of undress having his wicked way with a maid. I'm not really sure who I'm supposed to be tonight, but I'm wearing it with simple black trousers. Benedict, I guess. However, I know who Jackson is.

He's my whole world.

"Princess," I say urgently from the foot of the bed. "I couldn't let you marry that monster. He might be rich, but he doesn't love you."

"What would you know about love?" he spits back, a beautiful blush on his cheeks from his arousal.

I walk around the bed, my heart threatening to thump its way right out of my chest. I manage not to fidget as I stand beside him and gently take his hand. I'm glad he doesn't snatch it away. I wouldn't blame him, considering the scenario, but maybe he senses something is slightly amiss with this particular role play.

"I know that I love you, princess, with my whole heart. I might only be a simple scholar"— Oh, there we go. Yes, that fits perfectly —"but I will love you for the rest of my life and cherish you for all of our days. We will be poor, but we'll be rich with true love."

He's gone still, and I can't blame him. So I don't waste any more time.

I fish the ring box out of my trousers and get down on one knee.

Jackson's jaw drops, and his eyes are wide and shiny. I swallow down the last of my nerves and open the box. It's a beautiful band of rainbow gems set delicately into a rose gold ring. Pretty and sparkly, just like my beautiful boy.

"Jackson Travis Riggs," I manage to utter even though my throat is tight. "You are my princess. My pretty boy, my naughty girl, my everything. Being your Daddy and your partner is the best thing that's ever happened to me. But I think the most wonderful, miraculous thing would be to have the honor of being your husband. Will you marry me?"

I'm trembling slightly as I look up at him on the bed. Twin tears slide down his cheeks, and he places his hand on his heaving chest. "Are you really asking me to marry you, Benedict?" he whispers. "This isn't…part of the scene?"

"I'm really asking, baby boy," I say, grinning despite feeling like I'm going to pass out. "Will you spend the rest of your life with me and let me love you every single day?"

He shrieks and launches off the bed in a flurry of rose petals and swishing skirts. He lands on his knees before throwing himself at me, knocking us both over onto the carpet, peppering kisses all over my face.

"Yes, Daddy! Yes! Oh my god! Of course I'll marry you! This is the best day *ever!*"

I chuckle as I manage to untangle us enough to ease the ring out of its box and slide it onto his finger, breathing a sigh of relief when it fits. "Perfect," I murmur and straighten his tiara, which got knocked in his vault off the bed. "Just like you."

He bites his glossy lip and looks down at his hand, admiring the way the stones glitter in the glow from the fairy lights. "I love you so much," he says, shaking his head like he can't quite believe it.

"You wanted out and proud," I say to him, recalling his words from the airport last summer. "Well, there you go. Now the entire world will have no doubt that you belong to me, and I love you more than words can say. I will be your loyal servant until the day I die."

"You're quite the romantic for a brute, aren't you, Sir?" he says cheekily, flicking his eyebrows at me. "You know, I went to a lot of trouble to set all this up." He indicates the room, and my nerves are finally replaced by a surge of desire.

"I saw. Thank you, baby boy. This looks like the most perfect scene to ravish you for the first time as my fiancé."

He sighs and flutters his eyelids, placing his hands on his chest so the one with the ring is sparkling on top. "I suppose you *did* save me from marrying the wrong man. I guess I could reward you with a little ravishing."

"Is that so?" I tease, my hand drifting up his thigh toward the frilly garter.

"Yes, Sir," he says, those two magic words that started it all.

"Well, who am I to disappoint my princess?" I ask.

———

Thank you so much for reading Benedict and Jackson's story!

One jaded Daddy. One brand new boy. A fake relationship that becomes all too real.

Make sure you don't miss the next Paddle Creek College book featuring sweet Daddy, Ruben, and Xander, the stressed-out younger stepbrother of his best friend. Little Pleasures is coming April 2023.

Pre-order your copy now!

If you want more small towns or Daddies, make sure you keep reading for other books by HJ Welch/Helen Juliet.

———

If you'd like to be the first to know what's happening next in Paddle Creek, make sure to join my Facebook group, **Helen's Jewels.** We also have a lot of fun with games and giveaways, as well as ARC opportunities.

———

Thank you to my team!

Cover Design: Cate Ashwood

Editing: Meg Cooper (thank you for the car break down and Selena's special gift!)

Proof Reading: Tanja Ongkiehong

Formatting (and general awesomeness): Ed Davies

Love and support: Hubby and our cats

PADDLE CREEK #1: HEAVEN SENT BY HJ WELCH

Two rival jocks. One adorable nerd. A bet that changes everything.

SETH

Being captain of the Paddle Creek Panthers is my life. I wouldn't care that my grades have slipped, except it could not only cost me my shot at the pros, but now the rich kid in town has wagered that if I don't graduate, I'll owe him *big* time. Can this gorgeous little freshman geek Gabe really save my degree and my reputation? All I know is that as soon as I laid eyes on him, I needed him. And I *don't* want to share.

MARTY

I've spent almost four years trying to get my captain Seth to notice me. He's hot as hell and knows how to boss a guy around, even one as big as me. To him, though, I'm just the team clown. But when he drags me into this graduation bet, it's no laughing matter. So why shouldn't this little cherub Gabe tutor me as well? In fact, I don't see why we can't share him in all *kinds* of ways. Seth is clearly a natural Daddy, Gabe thrives being doted on, and I'm happy to Daddy *and* be Daddied. Win-win, right?

GABE

Somehow, I've found myself standing up to the guy whose family pretty much owns Paddle Creek and put my neck on the line for two of the college's star players. Now we're spending every day together as I try and save their grades, and I don't know if I'm crazy but it's like they both *want* me. I've never had a boyfriend. I'm not even out to my overbearing parents. How could I choose between them…or do I actually have to when they *both* want to be my Daddies? After my life comes crashing down, it's their turn to come to my rescue. Maybe what me and these god-like men have isn't just a fling after all?

*Heaven Sent is a steamy, standalone MMM romance. It's the first book in the **Paddle Creek College** series, where it's always the quiet ones who get up to the best kind of trouble. This book features a geek tutoring two hot jocks, two hot jocks tutoring a geek in a completely different way, a trash panda with a heart of gold, a human ice cream sundae, a revenge curse, and a guaranteed HEA with absolutely no cliffhanger.*

Click here to get the Heaven Sent eBook

he can't miss this opportunity, not even when his past comes back to haunt him.

————

Wild Ride

When Red is chased into the woods, he seeks sanctuary at his estranged grandma's house. He doesn't expect to be rescued by his older brother's best friend, the man he was always madly in love with. Could Hunter be the Daddy of Red's wildest dreams? Especially when he unlocks a secret passion of Red's for beautiful lingerie. There's still a threat lurking in the woods, though, and Hunter realises he'll do anything to protect his beautiful boy.

————

Three

When three shy best friends sign up to a dating app to finally get some by the end of the year, they don't expect to all fall for the same gorgeous, slightly scary-looking Daddy. The only solution? Let him choose who he wants to bed. Except he doesn't. Daddy Wolf wants to spoil each little piggy, one after another. But when danger comes calling, will their love for each other be enough to save them all?
Includes Halloween bonus scene!

————

Nine Lives

When Charlie suddenly finds himself homeless and penniless, he decides to sell the only thing left he owns. Himself. For the very first time. Lucky for him he stumbles across Miller, the own of a London kink club, who saves him from those who would take advantage of him. As Miller discovers his inner Daddy, he also unlocks Charlie's kitten alter-ego. But with both their families meddling, will new love be enough to keep them together?

Click here to get the Daddy's Fairy Tales eBook bundle

PINE COVE BOX SET BY HJ WELCH

Welcome to Pine Cove, where true love lives happily ever after! **This 2000 page box set contains all six novels as well as all five companion short stories.**

Click here to get the Pine Cove eBook bundle

Click here to get the Pine Cove audio bundle

———

Safe Harbor

Robin Coal needs a fake boyfriend for his high school reunion. He asks his housemate: a gorgeous, totally straight ex-Marine. What could go wrong? There's only one bed, and Dair might not be so straight after all... When Robin's past threatens their future, only Dair can save him.

———

Sweet Spot

It's Halloween and Robin has prepared a sexy little surprise for his boyfriend Dair when he gets home from work. Hold on to your horses, Marine!

————

Troubled Waters

Bodyguard Scout Duffy doesn't know what's worse: the fact that his scorching one-night-stand, Emery Klein, is his bratty new client, or the fact that he doesn't even remember Scout. But Emery's life is in danger thanks to his out and proud charity work, and once he finally recognizes Scout, their chemistry in undeniable.

————

Homeward Bound

Swift Coal just found out he's a father, and his daughter (and her cranky cat) are coming to stay. His best friend's younger brother, Micha Perkins, has nowhere to go and a wrongfully tattered reputation. He's relieved when Swift asks him to be a live-in babysitter. He just has to hide his lifelong crush. Easy, because Swift is straight—right?

————

Bright Horizon

With sixteen years between them, baker Ben Turner and lawyer Elias Solomon have no idea their crush is mutual. But when Ben inherits his long-lost family's estate and becomes an overnight millionaire, Elias swears to protect the innocent younger man from the vultures circling him. To unravel the mystery of the inheritance, they must go to England to confront Ben's estranged relatives...and their feelings for each other.

————

Crossed Paths

Raj Bhat is done living in the shadows. It's time for him to take charge of his own destiny and tell the man he's fallen for how he really feels.

———

Midnight Sky

It's the night before New Year's Eve. Taylan Demir is all alone, and he's just lost his dog. Except when his handsome customer, Hudson Perkins, comes to his rescue, Taylan doesn't just get his dog back. He's suddenly got a hot date, and maybe someone to kiss when the clock strikes midnight.

———

Memory Lane

Angel Shields saved Jay Coal's life in high school, and Jay has secretly loved his straight best friend ever since. Now Angel's back in town with amnesia after a suspicious work accident and it's Jay's turn to rescue him. He pretends to be Angel's fiancé to see him in the hospital, but with his scrambled-up memory, Angel's not sure it's fictional after all. He just knows he loves Jay more than ever.

———

Thin Ice

Kamran's ex broke his heart, tricked him into aiding a bank robbery, and now he wants him to do one last job. There's only one way to say no: seek the protective custody of the biggest, grumpiest FBI agent ever, Lee Marshall. And pretend to be his boyfriend for a week-long family reunion in their giant mansion. Wait, what?

———

Calm Shores

Gorgeous, sophisticated Dante walks into Oliver's bar and orders…a boyfriend?! Dante needs a man to keep his mother from setting him back up with his awful, cheating ex, and Oliver is up for the challenge.

————

Fresh Snow

Emery Klein is throwing the best Christmas party ever, but his fiancé, Scout Duffy, and all their friends have something more exciting in mind.

————

Each Pine Cove book can be read as a stand alone and has its own happy ever after. But if you read the whole series, you'll see a lot of familiar faces!

Click here to get the Pine Cove eBook bundle

Click here to get the Pine Cove audio bundle

HJ Welch is an author of contemporary MM romance series, including the international bestselling Pine Cove series. She lives just outside of London with her husband and two balls of fluff that occasionally pretend to be cats. She began writing at an early age, later honing her craft online in the world of fanfiction on sites like Wattpad. Fifteen years and over half a million words later, she sought out original MM novels to read. By the end of 2016 she had written her first book of her own, and in 2017 she achieved her lifelong dream of becoming a full-time author. When she's not writing she's usually dancing, singing, filming music videos, taking long walks, working on jigsaw puzzles, drinking prosecco, or talking about Eurovision.

She also writes contemporary British MM fairy tale adaptations as Helen Juliet.

————

You can contact Helen via the following:
Newsletter: https://www.subscribepage.com/helenjuliet
Website – www.hjwelch.com
Facebook Group – Helen's Jewels
Instagram – @helenjwrites
Twitter – @helenjwrites
Book Bub – @HJWelchAuthor
Facebook Page – @HJWelchAuthor

www.ingramcontent.com/pod-product-compliance
Lightning Source LLC
Chambersburg PA
CBHW051224210726
48290CB00003B/790